ME AND KATIE
(THE PEST)

ANN M. MARTIN

Drawings by Blanche Sims

ME AND KATIE
(THE PEST)

AN
APPLE
PAPERBACK

SCHOLASTIC INC.
New York Toronto London Auckland Sydney

The author would like to thank Prudence Morgan, Owner and Director of Centaur Farm Campus, Sergeantsville, New Jersey, for evaluating this manuscript.

ISBN 0-590-43618-X

12 11 10 9 8 7 6 5

4 5/9

Printed in the U.S.A.

28

For
MYRIAH LEIGH PERKINS
and
GABRIELLE ANN PERKINS
With Lots of Love

Contents

1.

Katie (the Pest)

Plunk, plunk, plunk. Plunkety-plunkety-plunk, plunk. Bam, bam, bam, bam. Plunkety-plunkety-plunk.

I yawned. Another piano recital. My little sister Katie was up on the stage in the recital room of the Riverside School of Music. She was playing a piece that I knew by heart. I knew it by heart because Katie had been practicing it at home for weeks.

Plunkety-plunkety-plunk.

I looked at my watch.

I squirmed.

I squinted my eyes to read the program. I wanted to see how many more kids had to perform before the recital was over.

Bam, bam, bam, bam.

I yawned again.

My mother poked me. "Pay attention, Wendy," she whispered. I pinched myself a couple of times and sat up straight.

Plunkety-plunkety-PLUNK!

Katie finished her song with a dramatic crash. She scooted off the piano bench and curtsied the way her music teacher had taught her. Then she smiled sweetly at the audience and ran off stage. She knew she'd win another award.

Katie is *always* winning awards. She has so many they make her bedroom sag. They cover her walls. If she wins an award today, it will be her fifth from the School of Music. And she's only eight and a half years old. She has four spelling medals, two science fair ribbons, and a second prize award from the place where she takes art classes. Plus she has a certificate for writing the best composition in all the third grade on why it's important to be a good citizen. She won a hundred dollars for that, too. (Mom and Dad made her open a savings account with it.)

Katie's been mentioned in our town paper twice this year. Next year, she'll probably win the Nobel Peace Prize or something.

I'm ten. (Well, actually nine years and eleven months.) I won a medal once. It was for having the cleanest desk in second grade. Big deal. The walls in *my* room are bare.

I've never been in the paper, except for when I was born. That doesn't count.

Here are the things Katie's good at:

> playing the piano
> spelling
> science
> writing
> drawing
> arts and crafts
> being a gigantic Pest

Here's what I'm good at:

> baseball
> acting
> talking
> taking out the garbage

I yawned again. I couldn't help it. The last little kid was at the piano now. He was six years old, playing "Row, Row, Row Your Boat."

When he finished, the audience clapped politely.

Then Mr. Neusome, Katie's teacher, said, "And now I would like to announce the winners of the awards for our Summer Piano Concert. Students?"

Katie and the rest of the music students filed on to the stage. They stood behind Mr. Neusome in an uneven line.

Mr. Neusome announced the winners in Class I (the beginners), then Class II, Class III, and finally Class IV, the most talented kids. Katie was in Class IV. She was the youngest one. And she won first prize. *First prize.*

Geez.

Another medal.

Someday her room is going to collapse under the weight of all those awards.

I slumped down in my seat. But everyone else was standing and clapping. Dad hauled me to my feet so I could join in.

Hooray. Yay.

When the excitement was over, Mom, Dad, Katie, our five-year-old brother Scott, our housekeeper Miss Johnson, and I walked outside to our cars. There were three of them. Cars, that is. This was because it was a Thursday morning and Mom and Dad had to go back to work. So Mom hugged Katie, got in her blue Chevrolet, and drove off. Then Dad hugged Katie, got in his red Ford, and drove off. Then Miss Johnson hugged Katie, herded us kids into the yel-

low Volkswagen Rabbit, and drove us home.

It was summer vacation, so we were free. I was freest of all. Katie was taking art lessons, piano lessons, and creative writing classes. (Her idea.) Scott was going to day camp three times a week. (Miss J.'s idea.) But I didn't have anything planned. (Nobody's idea. I just didn't know what to do with myself.)

Miss J. parked the car in our driveway. "Lunch time!" she said. "Fruit salad and yogurt."

Miss J. only feeds us healthy food. Most of the time it's okay. But sometimes I wish for Twinkies and Ring-Dings and Big Macs and Lucky Charms and Dr. Pepper. (Miss J.'s idea of a really terrific dessert is cheese wedges with apple slices.) Mom says we are very lucky to have Miss J., and not to complain. And I love Miss J. I really do. It's just that sometimes I get tired of Health.

Miss J. let us eat lunch at the picnic table in the backyard. While we were eating she went inside to watch "Love and Life" on TV. She takes a break every day at "Love and Life" time. (We never watch "Love and Life" with her because it's very boring. Just a lot of people talking and smooching.)

I was starving and finished my fruit salad before anyone else. Katie caught me eyeing this big strawberry that was in the middle of her plate.

She picked it up. "Mmmm," she said, licking her lips. "Mmmm." She took a teeny tiny bite out of it. "Oh, yum. That is soooo good." She closed her eyes.

I ignored her.

"Weren't your strawberries good, Wendy?" she asked. "Too bad you don't have any left."

I stuck my tongue out at her.

Katie took another nibble. "Mmmm. *Mmmm.*" She waved it in front of my eyes. "Too bad you were a pig."

I snatched at the strawberry and knocked it out of her hand. It fell under the picnic table.

"Meanie!" shrieked Katie. "Now it's covered with germs." She ran inside, probably to tattle.

I told you she was a gigantic Pest.

"Here, Wendy," said Scott. "You can have mine."

Scott is not a pest. (Usually.)

After lunch Miss J. made me stay in my room for a half an hour because I was mean to Katie. When the half hour was over, I ran next door to Sara Holland's house. Sara is my best friend. She's quiet and shy and thoughtful. And she doesn't have any brothers or sisters. Only cats. Their names are Star and Lucy. Sometimes I go to Sara's just for the peace and quiet.

I went in her back door (we never bother to knock) and found her where I knew I'd find her. Cuddled up in the den, reading. She was reading *Charlie and the Chocolate Factory* for the third time. Star was asleep in her lap.

"Hi!" Sara said. She put a bookmark in *Charlie*.

"Hi," I said glumly.

"What's wrong?" she asked.

"Katie," I replied. "She's being a gigantic Pest again." I told her about the strawberry and the punishment.

"And you know what else?"

Sara shook her head.

"She won another award today."

"You're kidding."

"Nope. At the music school. Her fifth for piano. It was a first place."

"Wow," said Sara. "Gosh." Then she added, "I'm sorry, Wendy."

See, Sara knows how I feel about Katie and her awards and being a gigantic Pest. And I know how Sara feels about being shy. Last month she had to be in our class play. I thought she was going to die! But I helped her with her lines and she survived.

"You know what?" said Sara, moving Star gently off her lap. She stood up.

"What?" I asked.

"*You* could win an award."

"*Me?* What for?"

"I don't know. *Do* something. Something important. There must be something you can do better than Katie."

"Oh, sure. I can take out the garbage better than she can. I can reach my tenth birthday faster than she can. I can—"

"Oh, come on. You know what I mean.... Well, we can think about it."

"All right."

"Hey, let's work on the saga. Then you could be in *The Guinness Book of World Records*. Katie hasn't done *that* yet."

Sara and I and Sara's cousin Carol who lives across the street are writing "The Saga of Barbie and Ken." It's the story of Barbie and Ken and their adventures and their seventeen children. The saga is over three hundred and ninety stanzas long. When we reach four hundred stanzas, we're going to send it to *The Guinness Book* to see if it breaks a record. We're sure it's the longest poem ever written by kids.

So we went over to Carol's house to work on the saga. But I knew my mind wouldn't be on writing and rhyming. I would be thinking of what I could do better than Katie.

There had to be something.

2.

Real Live Horses

"Look!" cried Ken.
"It's the dapple gray,
a fabulous steed!
We'll ride away
and find that crook
and he'll be sorry
about *every*thing he took!"

"Do you think that last line is okay?" asked Carol.
"It sounds sort of funny to me."

Sara chewed on her pencil. "I don't know . . ."

"The Saga of Barbie and Ken" was very exciting.
It was stanza #392, and Barbie and Ken were about
to catch a wicked bank robber. He had stolen mil-
lions of dollars in cash, and had run through the
countryside, scaring people right and left.

I pictured the dapple-gray horse in my mind. He was galloping across a wide field, his mane flying. And I was riding him bareback. I was bumping along with the wind in my face.

I liked horses. A lot. Recently I had started collecting horse things. I had two tiny china horses and six bigger horses and almost every single horse book Marguerite Henry ever wrote. My favorite was *Misty of Chincoteague*. I wished I were Maureen Beebe with a pony of my own. I would ride it every day.

"Hey! That's it!" I shrieked. I jumped off of Carol's bed. "That's it! That's it!"

"What's it?" asked Carol.

"I know something I can do that Katie never could!"

"What?" asked Sara excitedly.

"I can take horseback riding lessons! I love horses. But Katie's scared of them. She wouldn't get within two miles of one. And even if she did, she couldn't get on a horse's back. I mean, *mount* a horse," I corrected myself. "She's too uncoordinated."

This was true. Katie couldn't catch a football or hit a baseball. She couldn't stand on her head or do a backward somersault. It had taken her months just to learn to ride a bicycle.

"That's a great idea!" cried Sara.

"Oh, boy! I can't wait to ask Mom and Dad!" I

settled down on Carol's bed again, and tried to concentrate on the saga.

"Only eight more stanzas to write, and we can send it off again," commented Carol.

We had sent it off once before when it was just three hundred fifty stanzas long. Only we made a big mistake. We had wanted to send the saga to *The Guinness Book of World Records*. The author of *The Guinness Book* is Norris McWhirter, but I had told Carol and Sara that Norris McWhirter was a pen name for Sir Alec Guinness, the movie star. So we sent the saga to him. I was positive that Sir Alec Guinness wrote *The Guinness Book*. I mean, the names were the same and everything. But I was wrong. *Very* luckily, Sir Alec was nice enough to return the saga. He even wrote us a letter and said he thought we would be poetesses one day. We had decided to add fifty more stanzas to the saga, as long as we had it back. Then we would send it to *The Guinness Book* for real.

Now there were just eight stanzas to go. We had been working very hard. Maybe we could finish it tomorrow.

That night I had to wait forever before I could ask Mom and Dad about riding lessons. First Dad called Miss J. to say he'd be home late. Then Mom called to say she was stuck with one of her clients. (Mom is a lawyer.) When they finally got home, Miss J. wanted to serve dinner right away.

But at last I had Mom and Dad all to myself. Miss J. was in the kitchen, and Katie and Scott were getting ready for bed.

Mom and Dad were in the living room, reading the paper.

"Can I talk to you?" I asked them.

"Of course," Mom said, putting the paper down.

"I thought of something," I said. "I thought of something I'd really like to do this summer."

"Oh, what?" asked Mom, her eyes shining. I knew Mom had been worried because I didn't have any summer plans.

"I'd like to take horseback riding lessons. I really would. I—" I was going to add how much I loved horses and wished I were Maureen Beebe. But I didn't have to.

"That's a *won*derful idea!" said Dad.

Mom smiled. "I took riding lessons when I was your age. It was lots of fun. I've even got my old riding hat. Of course you can take lessons."

"Oh goody, goody, goody! Thank you, thank you, thank you!" I cried. "Real live horses! Where will I take lessons?"

"I'll find out tomorrow," said Mom. "We'll get you

enrolled as quickly as possible. Since it's already the beginning of July, classes may have started. But that shouldn't matter much."

The next day seemed like the longest day of my life. I couldn't wait for Mom to come home. I wanted to call her at the office and ask her if she had signed me up for lessons, but I didn't want her to think I was bugging her.

So I went over to Sara's. I found her roller skating on the driveway with Carol.

"Hey, you guys!" I yelled.

They rolled over to me.

"Guess what?" I cried.

"What?" asked Sara and Carol.

I practically exploded with my news. "I can take riding lessons!" I squealed. "Mom said so. She's finding out about them today."

"That's great!" said Sara.

"Yeah! . . . Do you want to get your skates?" asked Carol.

"No, let's finish the saga. Please, please, *please?* I'm getting nervous about riding lessons. Working on the saga will take my mind off waiting. Besides, we're so close to finishing."

Carol and Sara sat down and began unlacing their skates. When they had their running shoes back on, we went over to Carol's house. She got the saga from the hiding place in her closet. Then we dashed back to Sara's and closed ourselves into the den.

We sent Barbie and Ken off to the Mojave Desert for the last couple of stanzas. There they uncovered a cache of stolen rubies, and then were reunited with their seventeen children who had been kidnapped when their bus was hijacked. Ken rented nineteen horses, and they all rode off into the sunset for a happy ending.

"I don't believe it!" I cried, as Sara wrote the last word and threw her pen down. "It's finished! . . . Again."

Carol giggled. "Yeah. Four *hundred* stanzas. We did it!"

"Well, let's send it off," said Sara.

"Only this time we'll be more careful," I added. "First, we have to Xerox the whole saga."

"Okay," she agreed.

So we took our time. We wrote a letter to *The Guinness Book* people. Then we Xeroxed the saga at the library. We packaged it up carefully and took it to the post office.

Afterwards, I crossed and uncrossed my fingers seven times, hoping for good luck.

When Mom came home that evening, I pounced

on her. "Did you call? Did you find out about lessons?"

Mom smiled. "You're all set," she said. "You start on Tuesday."

"Oh, Mom!" I cried. I threw my arms around her. "I can't believe it! Thank you!"

It turned out that I would be taking lessons just outside of Riverside at stables called Hasty Acres. The Larricks owned the stables, and Mrs. Larrick and her daughter Paula gave lessons every day. Mom had enrolled me in a beginners' class. It met Tuesday and Thursday afternoons. I'd missed two lessons, but Mrs. Larrick said it didn't matter.

"There's even bus service," said Mom. "Mrs. Larrick's son Charlie drives a minibus. He'll pick you up right here at the house and bring you home after each lesson."

I nodded.

"Oh, and tomorrow," added Mom, "we'll go shopping. You'll need riding boots and jodhpurs. Maybe we'll get you a new shirt, too."

I was so excited I couldn't speak.

In just four days I, Wendy Matthews White, would ride a real live horse!

The next day, as she'd promised, Mom took me shopping. We bought a red and white plaid shirt, a pair of jodhpurs (special riding pants), and a pair of leather riding boots.

I looked at the riding hats. There was a gorgeous green one I wanted very badly.

Mom checked the price tag. "I'm sorry, honey," she said. "This is just *too* expensive. We've spent a lot of money already. If you like the lessons, maybe we can get it for your birthday. For now, you can wear my old hat. It's in the attic somewhere, I'm sure."

"Okay," I said.

As soon as we got home, I tried on the entire outfit. Mom's hat was sort of battered and dirty, but I didn't care. I stood in front of the bathroom mirror and decided I looked like a real horsewoman. I looked professional.

While I was admiring myself, Katie appeared in the mirror behind me. For a second she just stared. I could almost *see* her thinking.

"You got all that?" she cried. "All *that?* It's not even your birthday yet. Mommy bought you a whole outfit? I don't have any real outfits."

The Pest loves costumes. When she was little she liked to dress up. At first, Mom's old clothes were good enough for her, but soon Katie wanted to be a policewoman, a doctor, a cowgirl, an Indian. She

had all these costumes. But they were pretend. She wanted a real one.

"Mommy never bought *me* a real outfit," she fumed.

"I'm sure that means she doesn't love you as much as she loves me," I muttered, but the Pest didn't hear.

She stamped her foot and crossed her arms.

I turned around and faced her. Then I stamped my foot and crossed my arms.

The Pest stuck her tongue out.

I stuck my tongue out.

"Meanie-mo," she cried.

"Meanie-mo," I cried.

The Pest narrowed her eyes.

I narrowed my eyes.

"Copycat!" she shouted.

"Copycat!" I shouted.

She ran out of the bathroom. "I'm telling!"

I ran after her. "I'm telling!"

"Mommy!" she called.

"Mommy!" I called.

The Pest ran in the kitchen. "Mommy?"

I followed her. "Mommy?"

"Shut up, Wendy. Just shut up," yelled the Pest.

"Shut up, Wendy. Just shut up," I said.

"Ha ha. Now you're telling yourself to shut up."

"Ha ha. Now you're telling yourself to shut up."

"Leave me alone!" Katie's voice was rising. She was starting to sound hysterical.

"Leave me alone!" I yelled anyway. I let my voice rise, too.

"Mommy!" the Pest called down the basement stairs.

"Mommy!" I called, leaning down behind her.

No answer.

Katie went furiously into the living room, looked out the window, and saw Mom in the front yard, watering the rosebushes. "Oh, good. There she is."

"Oh, good. There she is."

I followed so closely behind the Pest that I stepped on her heel and her shoe came off. But that didn't stop her. She ran over to my mother with one bare foot.

"How come Wendy got all that stuff?" she whined.

"Those things are for her riding lessons," replied Mom, putting the hose down.

"But you never bought *me* an outfit."

"You have a piano for your piano lessons and an easel and paints and clay for your art lessons," Mom said patiently. "Those are for Wendy."

"But I want an outfit."

"You have more costumes than you know what to do with," said Mom.

"Get her a pig outfit," I suggested.

"Wendy!" exclaimed my mother. "That's enough." She gave me a look. It meant "For heaven's sake, be nice to your sister."

The Pest ignored us. "I don't mean costumes like those. Not cowgirls and ballerinas. I want a real outfit—for one of my lessons."

"Such as what?" asked Mom.

"Such as . . . such as . . . a beret for my art lessons," answered the Pest triumphantly.

"We'll see," said Mom.

"How about a toad outfit," I said, "or a cockroach outfit?"

"That will do," said Mom very firmly. She gave me another look. This one meant "You're treading on thin ice, young lady."

The Pest went back in the house.

I followed her.

"You're a spoiled brat," she said.

"You're a spoiled brat," I said.

3.

Peanuts

"Gosh, you look terrific, Wendy," said Sara.

I was sitting on the curb in front of my house, wearing my jodhpurs, boots, the hat, and my new plaid shirt.

"Thanks," I said. I glanced up and down the street, looking for the minibus. I felt a teeny bit nervous, but I'd never admit it. Actually, I felt more than a teeny bit nervous. My stomach felt as if it were riding the Scrambler at the amusement park.

It was the day of my very first riding lesson. In less than an hour, I'd be on the back of a real live horse. I'd be riding it just like Maureen Beebe.

"Will you tell me all about the lesson?" asked Sara, sitting down beside me. "You can come over after supper tonight."

"Okay," I said.

"Here comes the bus! Here comes the bus!" called a shrill voice.

Katie. She'd been hiding behind the yew bush in our front yard. I swear, she is always spying on us.

"Thanks a lot, Pest!" I yelled.

Sara and I stood up. The bus pulled to a stop in front of us.

"'Bye!" called Sara

"'Bye," I said. I climbed in. Three other kids were there, two girls and a boy. They were talking and laughing. I guess they already knew each other.

I was the new kid.

I sat in an empty seat.

One of the girls smiled at me. "I'm Mandy," she said.

"Hi, I'm Wendy."

"And this is Vicky and this is Tom."

"And I'm Charlie Larrick," the driver said over his shoulder.

The van drove out of Riverside, along a country road with lots of green pastures and trees and cows. Finally I saw a wooden sign that said HASTY ACRES. We turned onto a gravel driveway. I stared out the window, looking for horses.

We reached the end of the drive, and Charlie parked

by a huge white farmhouse. Mandy opened the door and we scrambled out.

"Come on!" said Mandy. "I'll show you the stables." She grabbed my hand and pulled me across the drive, away from the house. We ran to a building that looked like a barn. The big double doors were open. And right in front of them was an absolutely beautiful horse. He was a deep brown color with a white star between his eyes. His mane and tail were jet black. He was standing patiently while a tall boy in a blue work shirt brushed his tail.

"Ooh," I said. I left Mandy's side and went so close to the horse that I was almost touching him.

The boy grinned at me. "You like her?" he asked.

So "he" was a "she."

"Oh, yes!"

The horse blinked her eyes. And then—I swear it—she smiled at me.

I smiled back, not even feeling silly for smiling at a horse.

"This is Peanuts," said the boy. "And I'm Chris. You must be Wendy White. This is your first lesson. Would you like to ride Peanuts today? She's very gentle."

"Oh, yes!" I said again, just as Mandy ran up and cried, "No fair! I wanted to ride Peanuts today."

"You know the rule," Chris told her. "First come,

first served. Why don't you ride Mr. Chips or Daybreak? You like them just as well. And Peanuts is
good for a first-time rider."

"All *right*," said Mandy grumpily.

Peanuts stood quietly while Chris groomed her.
She blinked her eyes in the warm sun, and shifted
her weight from one foot to the other. I couldn't
take my eyes off her.

Just as Chris was finishing with Peanuts, two car-
pools arrived, bringing six more kids. They chose
their horses, and after Chris had led the horses outside, he said we were ready to begin the lesson. He
helped us line up the horses and we walked them
away from the stable, along a dirt path, leading them
by their bridles. I couldn't help looking at Peanuts.
A couple of times she glanced back with her soft
brown eyes. She whuffled at me. I whispered to her.
"Good girl," I said. "You're a good girl, Peanuts."

Whuffle, whuffle.

Once she leaned over and whuffled right on my
neck. It made me giggle.

I think Peanuts liked me already.

The path opened onto a clearing in a wide grassy
field. A couple of riding rings were marked by white
fences. Further away I could see a jumping course.

I led Peanuts into the nearest ring, following the

other kids. Inside the ring, they lined the horses up side by side in a row across the middle.

A woman in an outfit like mine crossed the ring. "Good afternoon, class," she said. She looked at me. "Wendy White?" she asked.

I nodded.

"I'm Mrs. Larrick. You've missed a couple of lessons, but you'll catch up." Mrs. Larrick smiled at me and rubbed Peanuts's nose affectionately.

Peanuts shook her head and sneezed.

Everybody laughed.

"I'm sorry I'm late," a voice called suddenly.

I glanced behind Mrs. Larrick and saw a girl come running toward us across the ring. She looked a little older than Charlie, maybe twenty or so.

"Hi, Paula!" cried Mandy.

"Hi, Mandy. Hello, everybody," said Paula.

"Wendy, this is my daughter, Paula," Mrs. Larrick told me. "She'll help give the lessons. She's my best instructor."

"I'm her *only* instructor," Paula whispered to me. I smiled.

Mrs. Larrick stepped back. "Okay, class. Please mount your horses."

For just a second, I panicked. I looked up at Peanuts. Suddenly she seemed awfully tall. How was

I supposed to climb on her back? Maybe she'd be polite and stoop down for me.

But I didn't have to worry. Paula came over and put a wooden box in front of me. "Step up on the mounting block," she said. "Grab the saddle, put your left foot in the stirrup, and pull yourself up, swinging your right leg over. Use the strength in your legs."

I hoisted myself up in the stirrup and swung my leg over.

I was sitting on Peanuts!

"Terrific!" exclaimed Paula.

"Wendy, that was very good," said Mrs. Larrick. "You've never ridden before?"

"Nope." Maybe all the baseball had given me good leg muscles or something.

"That was excellent."

"Thank you," I said, suddenly shy.

I sat solidly on Peanuts. I liked the feel of her body underneath me. She seemed strong and sure of herself. She made me feel strong, too. I looked down. The ground seemed sort of far away. But I knew Peanuts wouldn't let me fall off. At least, I didn't think she would.

I leaned forward a little and stroked Peanuts's neck. I ran my hands through her mane. I almost expected her to purr, the way Sara's cats do when you pat them. But Peanuts just stood patiently, whuffling every now and then.

"All right, please form a line and walk your horses around the ring. Vicky, you lead off," instructed Mrs. Larrick.

When it was almost my turn, Paula appeared next to me. "Tell Peanuts to turn right by pulling on the right side of her reins. And kick her with your heels to make her start walking."

"*Kick* her?" I cried. "I can't—"

"It doesn't hurt her," said Paula. "It's a signal, like a traffic light. She knows what it means. She's used to it."

I hesitated.

"Come on, Wendy," said Tom, who was next to me. "I'm on Sky High and he doesn't like to wait. For anything."

"Yeah, he'll nip Peanuts's tail if you don't get going," called Mandy.

"Just remember that you're the boss," Paula told me. "*You* tell your horse what to do. *You* stay in control."

I drew in a deep breath and kicked Peanuts's sides while I pulled on her rein. Peanuts turned and began walking toward the fence. She didn't act as if I'd hurt her.

"That's it!" called Mrs. Larrick. "Good, Wendy!"

"And you're a good girl, too," I whispered to Peanuts. "I'm sorry I had to kick you."

Peanuts plodded along. Every step she took made her back rise and fall. I went up and down, side to side, softly and slowly. It was a little like being on a raft on the ocean.

Peanuts reached the fence and I pulled on the left side of her reins. She turned! Then she followed the other horses around the ring. Sky High and Tom were right behind us. Not too close, I hoped. I didn't want any tail-nipping going on.

"Keep your horse a good distance away from the one in front," Mrs. Larrick said to the class, as if she could read my mind. "Slow down if you have to. Just pull back a little on the reins."

For the rest of the lesson we practiced walking—starting and stopping and turning. Peanuts did exactly what I told her to do. I just had to remember that I was in control.

I decided I was very glad I was riding Peanuts and *not* riding Sky High. Sky High was a huge horse, taller than any of the others. (I guess that's how he got his name.) And he was skittish. He didn't always obey. He'd go dancing out of line. Or he'd stop suddenly and stretch his neck down to snack on some grass. And once he very nearly did nip

Peanuts's tail. Tom was always having to kick Sky High or stop him or pull his head up. Sky High was walking trouble.

Peanuts was an angel. When the lesson was over, she glanced back at me as if to say, "How'd I do?"

"You did great!" I told her, leaning over to hug her neck. "And I'm glad nobody nipped your tail. Sky High needs to go to charm school."

After the lesson, we led our horses back to the stables. Paula walked with me and we talked the whole way. She was a Marguerite Henry fan, too!

When we reached the stables, I handed Peanuts over to Chris.

"How was your lesson?" he asked.

"Oh, it was terrific!"

"She's a pro, Chris," said Paula. "She's going to be a good rider."

"Peanuts is the best," I said. I wished I had a horse of my own, just like Peanuts.

"She's a good old horse," agreed Chris.

"Old?" I repeated.

"Yeah. She's about the oldest horse here. . . . Oh, but don't worry," he added. "She's got a few good years left in her." He rubbed Peanuts's neck.

She whuffled and shook her head.

"Well, 'bye, Peanuts," I said.

She stretched her neck toward me.

"Next time I'll bring you a carrot," I called, as I raced for the bus.

I was the last one on. I slumped into a seat.

Mandy didn't seem mad about Peanuts anymore. "Let's sing 'They Built the Ship Titanic,'" she cried, as Charlie turned the bus around.

"Oh, no, please," moaned Charlie. "Anything but that."

We sang it anyway, and 'John Jacob Jingleheimer Schmidt' and 'The Ants Go Marching' and a bunch of other songs.

When we reached my house, I leaped off the bus, calling good-bye to everyone.

Then I ran inside to tell Miss J. about the lesson. It had been one of the best afternoons of my entire life.

4.

The Pest Strikes Again

"Guess what!" I announced. I was sitting at the table with my family. Miss J. had just served us dinner.

"What, lamb?" asked Dad.

"Riding class was great! I rode this nice horse named Peanuts. She likes me already. She's brown with a white star between her eyes. I mounted and dismounted all by myself. And I rode her around the ring. You don't know what it feels like to be up on a horse. It's wonderful!"

"Honey, I'm so pleased," said my mother. She and Dad were grinning. "I'm really glad you've found something you enjoy."

"I wish I owned a horse," I said.

Mom and Dad glanced at each other, then continued eating.

Scott smiled at me from across the table. "Know what? Tomorrow we get pony rides at camp," he said. "Just like you."

"That's good," I said. "You'll have fun, Scottie."

I noticed that Katie was very quiet. She stirred her peas around her plate. Then she buried them under her mashed potatoes. She wasn't looking at any of us.

"Did you wear your boots and jodhpurs, Wendy?" she asked finally.

"Yes," I said. I was growing suspicious.

"Mommy," Katie said suddenly, "can I take riding lessons, too? I really want to."

"Do you have *time?*" Mom asked.

"Mom, NO!" I shouted. I slammed my fork down on my plate.

"Wendy," warned Dad.

"No fair! She can't take riding lessons, too."

"Well, honey—" Mom began.

"Don't let her! Don't let her!" I cried. I wanted to run upstairs to my room. But I stayed so I could see what would happen.

"Katie, I thought you didn't like horses," said my father.

"Yeah, they're big and scary, Pest," I said.

"I am not a pest," replied Katie. "And anyway,

you said Peanuts was nice. Not big and scary. You said she likes you and—"

"Oh, shut up."

"That'll do, Wendy," said Mom. "Katie, you're already taking three different kinds of lessons. How are you going to fit riding in, too?"

"I don't have any lessons on Tuesday or Thursday afternoons," answered Katie. "And that's when Wendy's lessons are, right?"

"Right," agreed my mother slowly.

"So can I?" Katie asked again. "Can I take riding, too? You let Wendy. And I really, really, really, really want to learn to ride."

"Oh, *Mom*." How could I explain why I didn't want Katie in my class? She was going to ruin everything for me. She'd probably get over being uncoordinated and turn into a champion rider before our very eyes. She'd win two thousand medals and cups, and we'd have to keep them in the garage so her bedroom floor wouldn't give way and send Katie crashing through it into the laundry room.

"Wendy, what's wrong?" asked my mother.

"I don't want Katie in the same class with me. Can't we take separate lessons?"

"*Why* don't you want Katie in your class?" asked Dad.

"I—I just want to do something on my own, that's

all." I wasn't going to say that I thought Katie was better than I was. Not with Katie sitting right there at the table. And I certainly wasn't going to let on that I planned to win a prize this summer just so I could show everyone *I* was good at something, too. It would spoil the surprise if it actually happened.

"Well," said Mom, "I guess I can understand that. There must be more than one beginners' class. And since Charlie picks you up on the bus, it's not as if it's any extra trouble for Miss J. if you two go out to Hasty Acres separately. All right, Katie. You can take lessons. We'll see if Mrs. Larrick can squeeze you in another class. But since you're taking so many other lessons, and since they're expensive, you'll have to wait awhile before we buy boots or jodhpurs. You can ride in your hiking boots and jeans. We'll find a secondhand hat somewhere."

Katie looked disappointed, but I didn't bother to gloat. Everything was practically ruined.

Right after dinner I went over to Sara's.

She was swinging in the hammock and I climbed in with her.

"How was your lesson?" she asked. "Did you really ride a horse?"

"I really did," I said. For a minute I forgot about Katie. "It was so much fun! I rode this horse named

Peanuts. She's old, but she's pretty and nice and does whatever you tell her. I think she likes me."

"How can you tell?"

"She smiled at me. And she kissed me, sort of."

"With horse lips?" screeched Sara. "Ew, ew, ew."

"No, it wasn't gross," I giggled. "And I learned how to get on her and off her without any help, and how to start her and stop her and make her turn. We rode around a ring in a field."

"Wow . . ." Sara sounded impressed.

"But guess what."

"What?" asked Sara.

"Katie's already ruined everything."

"She *has*? How?"

"She wants to take lessons, too."

"Oh, no!" cried Sara. "With you?"

"Maybe," I replied. "It depends on how many beginners' classes there are. She might end up with me."

"But she might not."

"But she might."

I sighed.

Sara sighed.

"What are you going to do?" asked Sara. "I mean, if she ends up in your class."

"I'm going to kill her."

"No, really," said Sara. "What will you do?"

I thought for a few seconds. "Get even," I finally replied.

"How?"

"I don't know. Yet. But I'll think of something." I paused. "Will you help me?"

Sara didn't answer right away. She thinks I'm mean to Katie sometimes. She and Katie aren't friends or anything, but Sara doesn't like to see people cry or get their feelings hurt. And since I'm older than the Pest, Sara isn't always on my side when I get after Katie.

"I'll think about it," said Sara at last.

From Sara, that was almost a "yes." She must have decided Katie was being pretty rotten.

"We could short-sheet Katie's bed," I suggested, "or mix up her paints, or hide those awards of hers somewhere—like in the trash compactor."

Sara narrowed her eyes at me. "I haven't made up my mind yet," she said.

"Okay, okay."

I stuck my leg out of the hammock and gave us a big push off the ground. Back and forth we swung.

It was getting dark out.

"Wendy!" Mom called from our back door.

"Ten more minutes?" I asked.

"All right," Mom agreed.

Sara and I swung slower and slower until we had

almost stopped moving. I caught a firefly and trapped it between my cupped hands.

"Well?" I asked Sara, watching the tiny light blink on and off.

"Well," said Sara. "Okay. I'll help. But only if we don't do anything *too* mean."

"Thanks," I said. We started the hammock up and swung until Mom called me in again.

The next evening when Mom came home from work, I was waiting for her just the way I had been last week. Only this time I wasn't excited. I was nervous. I was sulking on the front stoop as she came up the walk.

"Hi, honey," she said. She sounded tired.

"Hi."

Before I could ask about Katie's lessons, Katie burst through the front door.

"Did you ask?" cried the Pest. "Can I take lessons?"

Mom nodded. She sat on the stoop next to me. "You're in the beginners' class."

"Oh, yippee! Hooray!" The Pest whooped around the front yard.

"Is she in *my* beginners' class?" I asked. I crossed and uncrossed my fingers seven times, hoping the answer was no.

Mom nodded again. She put her arm around me. "I'm sorry, Wendy. I think I know how you feel. There's one other beginners' class, but it's jam packed. Mrs. Larrick said they absolutely couldn't put another student in it. Your class is smaller, so that's where Mrs. Larrick put Katie."

I stood up, shaking Mom's arm off me. "If the Pest is taking lessons, then I'm quitting," I announced.

Katie stopped her whooping and looked at me with hurt eyes.

I saw Mom's face change. "Well," she said briskly, "if you think that's best. You can give your riding outfit to Katie. At least it won't go to waste."

"Oh, no!" I cried. "No way. I'm not giving her my things. I'll stick with the lessons. You'll see. . . . But I bet Katie will drop out."

· With that, I stormed off to my room.

5.

Sky High

On Thursday, instead of getting on the bus to Hasty Acres by myself, I had to drag Katie the Pest along with me. Charlie and the kids said hi to me, then they all looked at Katie.

Here's another thing about Katie. She's really cute. Well, all right, she's pretty. She's tiny with a little heart-shaped face framed by blond hair, and she has these huge brown eyes and long black eyelashes.

Katie was the littlest kid on the bus and everyone thought she was adorable, especially after she told all her knock-knock jokes. First, Charlie started calling her Cutie. Then, Mandy taught her the bus songs we'd sung on Tuesday. And Tom slipped her a piece of bubble gum.

I sat by myself in the backseat with my arms

folded across my chest. I stared out the window, hating Katie. By the time we arrived at Hasty Acres, I had an idea for a great way to start getting even with the Pest. And Sara wouldn't even have to help me.

As soon as Charlie stopped the bus, I grabbed Katie. "Come on!" I cried. "I'll show you the stables and the horses." I raced ahead.

"Hi, Chris," I called when I reached the stables. "I'm the first one here. Can I have Peanuts again?"

"Sure thing, Champ," he said. "I'll get her saddled up for you." He disappeared inside just as Katie caught up with me.

"Come on in," I said to her. "I'll help you choose a horse. The rule is first come, first served. You can have whatever horse you want as long as you claim it before anyone else does."

"Okay," agreed Katie.

We walked into the dark stable. After our eyes adjusted to the light, I could see the horses' names on their stalls.

I took Katie's arm. "I know just the horse for you," I said. "Perfect for the first-time rider."

Katie beamed at me. She wasn't used to my being so nice to her.

Ha. She'd learn.

"But hurry before the other kids come or they'll get him first," I added.

At that moment, Mandy, Vicky, Tom and two other kids came into the stable. When they saw Peanuts being saddled they knew she was taken. They began clambering for Mr. Chips and other favorites.

"Hurry," I said again to Katie. I pulled her over to Sky High's stall. "This horse'll be great for you. Now stand right here, or someone else will probably get him. I've got to go stay with Peanuts while Chris saddles the horses."

I stood outside the stables loosely holding Peanuts's bridle. Peanuts whuffled and breathed on my neck, and I fed her a carrot I'd brought along. But I was mostly paying attention to what was going on in the stable.

Katie was waiting by Sky High's stall door. Chris saddled up Mr. Chips, Daffodil, Sundance, Eugene, and Daybreak for the other kids. They led them outside and stood with me.

Chris reached Katie. "Are you Katie White? Wendy's sister?"

Katie nodded.

"Ever ridden before?"

Katie shook her head.

Chris looked around at the stalls. "Let's see. Who'd be good for a beginner?"

"Sky High," answered Katie. "I want to ride Sky High."

"Sky *High?*" exclaimed Chris. He looked a little startled. "Are you sure?"

"Yes," said Katie definitely.

"I don't think that's a very good idea. How about—"

"No!" cried Katie, stamping her foot.

"Well . . . we'll see what Mrs. Larrick says. You can lead him to the riding ring."

Chris saddled Sky High and led him outside for Katie.

Katie stood beside me, looking up at her horse. It was a long way up. A very long way up. Sky High snorted and pawed the ground impatiently.

"Hold on to his bridle," I told Katie.

"His what?"

"His bridle." I showed her how I was holding Peanuts's bridle. Peanuts smiled at me (I think) and munched away at the last of her carrot.

Katie reached gingerly for Sky High's bridle. Sky High tossed his head and opened his eyes wide. The bridle jerked out of Katie's grasp and she jumped back. "Wendy . . ." she wailed.

I was a little afraid myself, but all I said was, "Oh, for pity's sake." That was what our father said when he thought we were being unreasonable.

"Let's go, gang," called Chris. "Everybody's here." He came over to give Katie a hand, so I walked ahead with Mandy.

When we reached the riding ring we lined the horses up like last time. I saw Chris whispering to Mrs. Larrick before he went back to the stable.

Then Mrs. Larrick and Paula walked to the middle of the ring. Paula and I smiled at each other.

After Mrs. Larrick introduced herself and Paula to Katie, she said, "Katie and Mandy, I'd like you to switch horses. I want you on Daybreak, Katie."

"Oh," groaned Mandy.

Katie glanced at me. I had told her Sky High was good for beginners. "Please, can't I ride Sky High?" she asked, not knowing why Mandy had just groaned.

"Katie—"

Mrs. Larrick started to say something, but just as she did, the Pest accidentally kicked Sky High's foot. He jumped to attention and bolted out of the line, dragging Katie beside him for several feet.

"Let go of his reins!" commanded Mrs. Larrick.

The Pest dropped them immediately and stumbled to the ground.

It was all over in just a few minutes.

Mrs. Larrick caught Sky High and walked him around the ring to calm him down.

Paula helped the Pest to her feet and talked to her for awhile to calm *her* down.

Then Mrs. Larrick led Sky High to the end of the line of horses, and in her most no-nonsense voice, told Mandy to come take his bridle. Mandy grumbled, but did what Mrs. Larrick asked.

Paula and the Pest walked over to Daybreak.

"Are you scared?" I heard Paula ask. "You could just watch today, if you like."

Katie shook her head. She did look scared, but nothing was going to keep her from riding lessons.

"Class!" Mrs. Larrick called for our attention, and told us to mount our horses.

I mounted Peanuts easily and watched Paula and Katie. Paula explained how to mount. She put the mounting block in front of Katie and told her just what she had told me last week. Katie got her left foot in the stirrup all right. And that was it. She couldn't pull herself up. She held onto the saddle for dear life. She pulled and pulled, but the only thing that happened was that the saddle slid over sideways slightly.

"Oof," groaned Katie.

Paula righted the saddle. "Let's try again," she said.

It was no good. Paula lifted her up partway, but not high enough. Finally Mrs. Larrick and Paula managed to sit Katie on Daybreak. After a few seconds, she actually looked fairly comfortable. Comfortable enough to turn her head and stick her tongue out at me. I stuck mine out at her.

Finally the lesson started. Once again, I rode around the ring on Peanuts. I sat up tall, holding the reins loosely, the way Paula had shown me last week. Peanuts did just what I told her.

And Daybreak did *some* things Katie told him. But Katie didn't have much control. And she still looked afraid. She sat all hunched forward gripping the reins, the saddle, anything. When she kicked Daybreak, she lost her balance and nearly fell off.

Katie was taking riding lessons all right, but she was *terrible*. For the first time in her life, Katie was really bad at something. I was better than she was! I probably didn't have to worry about her at all. What a relief.

I couldn't decide whether to be glad her lesson was going so badly, or mad because Paula spent the entire hour helping Katie. I didn't need any help, but it would have been nice just to talk to Paula.

When the lesson was over, we dismounted—except for Katie. Paula and Mrs. Larrick had to haul her off Daybreak.

I smirked.

Katie's first riding lesson was going to be her last.

6.

A Horse of My Own

I was wrong about the Pest. She went back to riding class on Tuesday.

And she got Peanuts.

The little sneak.

When Charlie picked us up she plunked herself down in the front of the bus, right next to the door. As soon as we parked by the farmhouse, Katie frantically opened the door, jumped out of the bus, and tore off to the stables. She got going in such a hurry that she beat everyone else there. By the time I arrived, Chris was saddling Peanuts for her.

The Pest smiled at me triumphantly.

"Hello there, Wendy," called Chris cheerfully.

"Hi," I said. I didn't feel cheerful at all. "Can I ride Mr. Chips?" I asked. No horse would be as good as Peanuts, but Mr. Chips seemed nice enough. What if I couldn't ride any horse except Peanuts, though? What if she were magic or something? Maybe I wasn't really a good rider after all.

Chris saddled Mr. Chips for me, and I led him outside. I led him as far away from Katie as I could get. Mr. Chips and I just stood for awhile. He didn't smile or kiss me or whuffle into my neck, but he didn't toss his head or snort, either.

I pulled a sugar cube from my pocket, put it on my palm, and held my hand out flat toward Mr. Chips. Mr. Chips blinked a couple of times, then very delicately took the cube between his lips. He crunched away contentedly, glancing at me every so often. I think Mr. Chips was shy.

When the lesson began a few minutes later, I mounted Mr. Chips as easily as I had mounted Peanuts. That was a relief.

Then I turned to watch the Katie-the-Pest Show. But it wasn't as good as I'd thought it would be. Katie actually managed to get on Peanuts all by herself. Not very gracefully, but she did it. And as soon as she did it, she looked straight at me and made a face.

I pretended I didn't see her.

We began walking around the ring. Katie didn't look as awful as she had on Thursday. Unfortunately. And I decided that Mr. Chips was just as good a horse as Peanuts (or maybe I *was* a good rider). He did what I told him. The only thing was, he seemed a little bored.

But not for long.

We'd been around the ring several times when Mrs. Larrick said, "Bring your horses to a stop, class."

We all put on the brakes, even Katie.

"You're doing beautifully, class," Mrs. Larrick said, "I think you're ready to begin trotting."

Trotting! The first thing I thought was, "Wait till I tell Sara." The second thing was, "Now maybe Katie will drop out."

We watched as Paula borrowed Daybreak from Mandy, kicked him into a walk, and dug her heels in again to speed him up to a trot.

Then she demonstrated posting. She stood slightly, lifting herself a few inches above the saddle, then sat, then stood, then sat, then stood. Up and down, up and down, in the rhythm of Daybreak's gait.

After that, Paula gave Daybreak back to Mandy, and helped to organize us in a tight line that stretched about halfway around the ring. I was at the head of the line.

"Okay, Wendy, you're first," called Mrs. Larrick.

"See if you can kick Mr. Chips into a trot, then trot around the ring to the end of the line."

I realized I was nervous. I wanted to do well, especially with Katie there. And I wished, for about the eighty-seventh time, that I were riding Peanuts. But the Pest had taken care of that.

I took a deep breath and let it out slowly. Then I kicked Mr. Chips. He walked a few steps and I kicked him again. The next second I was being bounced in the air. I felt as if I were riding in a car along a street full of potholes.

Bump, bump, jolt.

I stood in the stirrups to avoid the bouncing, then sat for a few seconds to rest my legs, then stood again.

"Terrific, Wendy!" cried Mrs. Larrick. "You'll be posting in no time."

We practiced trotting for the rest of the hour. Even Katie tried. When the lesson was over, I was so excited I could hardly hold still. I dismounted, kissed Mr. Chips on the neck, and jumped up and down a few times.

Paula came over and put her arm around me. "What did I tell you? You're a pro."

I beamed. "Thanks," I said.

"I'm serious," continued Paula. "You're really very

good. You've got good balance and poise, and nice control of your horse. You might want to consider taking private lessons as well as the group lessons. If you do, just let my mother or me know, okay?"

"O-*kay!*"

At dinner that night I told everyone what Paula had said.

"Honey, I'm so proud of you!" Mom smiled at me.

"That's fantastic," Dad said.

"Yay!" cried Scottie.

"Can we get a horse?" I asked.

"Oh, lamb!" laughed Dad.

Katie was drinking her milk and gazing out the window.

"How do *you* like lessons?" asked Mom.

Katie swallowed and choked on her milk.

Mom looked at her carefully. "*Do* you like riding lessons?" she asked.

"Yeah, they're fine," said the Pest.

"Are you sure?" asked Dad.

"Yup," said Katie. She took a big bite out of her hamburger and chewed it for a long time.

"Well . . . good," said Mom uncertainly.

* * *

That night I was getting ready for bed when I heard the Pest say to my mother, "Mommy, can I talk to you?"

"Of course, sweetheart," said Mom. They went into the Pest's bedroom and closed the door.

Immediately, I reached under my bed and pulled out a glass that I keep in a Florsheim shoe box. I keep it there for occasions just like this. I put the open end of the glass up to the wall that was between Katie's room and mine, and smushed my ear against the bottom of the glass.

I could hear Mom and the Pest talking, but not very clearly. So I got out the stethoscope my uncle Joe the doctor had given me. I tried listening with that, but it was even worse.

I went back to the glass.

"But," I could hear Katie say, "she never lets me play with . . . and she . . . I'm a pest."

The words faded in and out, but I could hear enough. I knew Katie was talking about me.

". . . she's older than you are and . . . her own friends. You . . . friends of your own," Mom was saying.

Right on, Mom.

"But I want Wendy to like me," I heard the Pest say quite clearly.

I pressed my ear even harder against the glass. I didn't want to miss Mom's answer.

"What do you mean . . ." The rest of the sentence was lost when Scottie flushed the toilet.

Darn.

"I . . . her to . . . play with Sara . . . always yelling at me."

"Why do you suppose she yells at you?"

"She says I spy on her and . . ."

"Do you?"

"Well, sometimes."

There was a long silence in the Pest's bedroom.

Then I heard Mom say, "Honey, you have to make an effort, too. . . . If . . . doesn't like you to spy on . . . don't do it . . . know it's hard, but . . . two-way street."

The old two-way street story. I'd only heard that about fifteen thousand billion times myself. It was Mom's way of saying that any argument takes at least two people, and that neither one is completely right or completely wrong. In other words, the Pest couldn't blame everything on me.

I was glad to know Mom felt that way.

I wished I hadn't found out by eavesdropping with a glass. I would have liked to have said something to my mother.

I put the glass back in the shoe box and shoved

the box under the bed. For a long time I sat and thought.

On Thursday, I managed to get Peanuts for my fourth lesson. The other kids were finding their own favorite horses by now. Mandy liked Daybreak and Mr. Chips, Vicky liked Eugene, and Tom like Sundance, a high-spirited young horse. (Nobody liked Sky High.) Katie, of course, tried to claim Peanuts again, just because she knew I wanted her. But she ended up with Daffodil.

I was on to Katie's tricks, so I easily beat her to the stables.

"Hi, Chris! Oh, *hi* Peanuts!" I cried. I dashed to Peanuts's stall.

Peanuts poked her head over the door and whuffled. I gave her a sugar cube and kissed the star between her eyes. When she finished the sugar she nuzzled me for more, stretching her neck out, and blowing on me.

My lesson that day was the best ever. We trotted around and around the ring, and I began to feel the rhythm for posting. Mr. Chips had been a good horse to ride, but I felt as if I understood Peanuts—and she understood me. And Mrs. Larrick told me in front of the whole class that I was an excellent rider, and that Peanuts and I made a good team.

Hardly anybody ever told me I was an excellent anything. And Mrs. Larrick said it right in front of Katie. The only thing was, Katie hadn't done too badly at this lesson herself. She had mounted Daffodil without a hitch. She sat more easily in the saddle. Paula was spending a lot of time with her and it seemed to be helping. Once, when we were trotting, Mrs. Larrick had even called out, "Very good, Katie." So how come it took the Pest three months to learn to ride a bicycle and only three *lessons* to learn to ride a horse? Was she getting more coordinated? I crossed and uncrossed my fingers seven times, hoping she wasn't.

"Dad?" I asked. It was Saturday morning and Dad was hovering around a flower bed in the front yard. He loves to garden. He was pulling up weeds and spreading peat moss.

I was lying on my back near the garden, chewing on some grass and looking at the clouds.

"Dad, could we get a horse? A nice, gentle one? It wouldn't be any trouble. We could keep it in the garage."

"Where would we put the cars?"

"Park them in the carport?"

"All *winter*?" Dad knelt by a peony bush and patted some peat moss around it.

"I don't know," I said.

"I'd like a horse, too," said a voice from behind the yew bush. The Pest was spying again.

"Well, we'll see," said Dad absentmindedly.

It was when the mail came that afternoon that I found the horse catalog. It was addressed to Mom and it was full of things you'd need if you owned a horse—grooming tools, brushes, buckets, riding clothes, and a lot more.

What did it mean? Were Mom and Dad really thinking about getting me a horse? As a surprise? Just in case they were, I slipped the catalog to the bottom of the pile of mail, and pretended I hadn't seen it.

That night I got out my birthday list. In one week I would turn ten. Mom and I had a party all planned. Carol, Sara, and another friend of ours named Jennifer were going to come for a sleepover.

I had asked Mom if the Pest had to come to the party. She said no, not if I didn't want her to. Mom really understands how I feel about Katie.

So the party would be me and Sara and Carol and Jennifer. We were going to make popcorn and watch a scary movie on TV and raid the refrigerator and not go to sleep at all.

I read over my birthday list, all the presents I'd asked Mom and Dad for. I'd given them the list weeks ago, but now I wanted to put one more thing on it.

With my fancy pen that wrote in sparkly gold ink, I added to the bottom of the list:

A HORSE OF MY OWN (please please please)

I wanted to make sure Mom and Dad knew how much I really, really wanted a horse. In case they still had some doubts.

7.

"Happy Birthday to You"

My tenth birthday fell on Saturday. For once. Saturday is the best day of the week for a birthday. If your birthday lands on a Wednesday or something it's no big deal. Your parents give you a couple of presents, and then you have to wait three days for your party. Only then it's not your birthday anymore, so what's the point?

But my tenth birthday was going to be great. Mom and Dad woke me in the morning. They came into my room singing "Happy Birthday." They brought me breakfast in bed. There was even a vase with a rose in it on the tray. Scottie climbed in bed with me and shared my toast.

The Pest was nowhere to be seen.

After breakfast I got dressed and went downstairs.

"Present time!" called Mom. "We thought you'd like to open your family presents now."

She took me out to the back porch. It was decorated with crepe paper and balloons. On the table was a stack of presents. Dad and Katie and Scottie and Miss J. were all waiting for me. They sang "Happy Birthday" again.

The Pest had a funny look on her face. I couldn't decide whether she looked guilty or smug or jealous or what. Maybe she was trying to keep a secret—a secret about a horse.

I opened the presents from Mom and Dad first. They gave me two more books by Marguerite Henry, *Album of Horses* and *Brighty of the Grand Canyon (Brighty* was actually a story about a burro, but that was okay), and my very first bikini. It was blue with yellow and green polka dots.

"Oh, how pretty!" exclaimed Miss J.

"Pretty," echoed Scott.

"Yeah," said Katie.

"You'll look gorgeous!" said Mom.

"Isn't it awfully . . . small?" asked Dad.

Then Miss J. gave me her present. Inside a small box was a gold chain with a tiny gold horse on it. "Oh, thank you!" I cried. I gave her a hug and a kiss, and fastened the chain around my neck.

Then Scott ran off the porch and returned holding

a rumply object. He handed it to me. It was something heavy wrapped up in tin foil. I carefully peeled
the layers of foil away and found a blob of clay. It
looked a little like a tall turtle with three ears, and
a leg coming out of its side.

"Scottie! How nice," I said. "*Thank* you! I'll put
it on my bookshelf."

"You know what it is?" he asked.

I didn't, but I hoped he'd tell me before I had to
ask him.

"It's a stegosaurus," he told me proudly.

Scott was learning about dinosaurs at day camp.
He loved dinosaurs as much as I loved horses.

And then the Pest gave me her present. I felt sort
of funny taking it from her, since I'd been so mean
and tried to make her ride Sky High, when all along,
the Pest just wanted me to like her. On the other
hand she was mean to me pretty often; I guess when-
ever she thought I wasn't being enough of a friend
to her. Maybe the present would be something awful. Last year, she was mad at me on Valentine's
Day and gave me a horrible, dirty brown heart that
said:

> Roses are red,
> Violets are blue,
> Snakes are ugly,
> And you are too.

Mom and Dad sent her to her room for doing that.

So now I took the present from her, not knowing what to expect.

"Thanks," I said. I glanced at her, but she was staring at the floor. She wouldn't look at me.

The package was small and flat and didn't weigh much. I slipped the ribbon off and tore away the paper to find a drawing of a horse. In fact, the horse was Peanuts—brown with a white star between her eyes.

"A picture of Peanuts?" I asked in surprise. "Where did you get it?"

"I drew it."

I told you Katie is good at art. The horse really looked like a horse. And horses are very hard to draw. I know. I've tried. Their legs are just about impossible to get right.

"Wow. Gee, thanks," I said awkwardly. It was the nicest gift she had ever given me.

"You're welcome," Katie told the porch floor.

"My goodness!" exclaimed my mother. She jumped up suddenly. "You know, I think there's one more present, isn't there?" she asked my father. "We've forgotten something."

A horse! Maybe they'd gotten a horse after all!

"Why, I believe you're right," replied Dad.

I giggled. They sounded so phony.

"Just something small," said Mom, but I could tell she meant the opposite. She dashed off the porch.

"Close your eyes, Wendy," said Dad.

"Yeah, close 'em," said Scott.

I closed them. I couldn't believe it. A horse? Really? Maybe they'd been hiding him in our garage. Or in Sara's garage. Her parents wouldn't mind.

I sat on the edge of my chair, quivering with excitement. When I opened my eyes, Mom might be standing in the backyard with a beautiful horse. Maybe it would even look like Peanuts. I hoped it would act like Peanuts, too. Not like Sky High.

"Okay!" said Dad. "Open your eyes."

I opened them very slowly. I wanted the horse in the backyard to appear in a blur as if I were having a dream. But I couldn't see a horse. I opened my eyes wide. No one was even in the backyard.

"What do you think?" Mom was asking anxiously. "It's the one you liked, isn't it?"

I realized that Mom was standing next to me, holding the gorgeous green riding hat from Pearce's that I'd wanted so badly.

I forced a smile onto my face. "Oh. Oh, yes. It's perfect. Thank you, Mom. Thanks, Dad." I kissed them both and then modeled the hat.

But I was very disappointed about the horse.

* * *

Later that morning I was in the hammock reading *Brighty of the Grand Canyon*, when out of nowhere came a voice.

I jumped a mile.

It was Katie. Why does she always have to sneak up on people? I hadn't heard her coming at all.

"Yikes!" I yelled. "What are you sneaking around for?"

"I'm not sneaking," said the Pest. "I wanted to ask you something."

"What?"

"Well," she said, "you like my present. Don't you, Wendy? You like the horse just a little, right?"

I softened. I remembered her telling Mom how much she wanted me to like her. "It's really nice," I said. "I like it a lot. I'm going to put Peanuts on the wall by my bed so I can look at her every night before I go to sleep."

"Really?" The Pest looked surprised and a little shy.

I was beginning to feel bad for giving her such a hard time. I knew she didn't *mean* to be a pest. She just wanted to be my friend. Mom once told me that since I was Katie's big sister she looked up to me.

"Yeah," I said. "Really. It was the nicest present you ever gave me."

Katie smiled.

"A lot nicer than the brown Valentine," I added.

Katie giggled.

Then she cleared her throat, looked down, and began tracing an arc in the grass with her right foot.

She was up to something again. I can always tell.

"Well, then," she began.

Oh, for goodness sake. Now what?

"Aren't you going to invite me to your party tonight?"

So that's what this was all about. The Pest wasn't being sensitive and sisterly. She just wanted an invitation to the party. She had put on a big act. She should win acting awards, too.

"NO!" I leaped out of the hammock and stomped into the house.

At six o'clock that evening the doorbell rang. I ran to answer it. Standing on the front porch were Sara, Carol, and Jennifer. They had all shown up at once.

"Happy birthday!" they shouted.

Carol was so excited she was jumping up and down. I let them in and they put their presents on the back porch.

We had dinner with my family at the picnic table outside. The party (the part Katie wasn't invited to) wouldn't start until after supper and cake and ice cream and presents.

Katie was still so mad at me that she wouldn't speak, and every time I looked at her she turned her head away. I started looking at her so often that she got too busy turning her head to be able to eat.

After dinner we gathered on the porch. Dad came out carrying a white bakery cake with eleven candles on it (ten, plus one to grow on), and everyone sang "Happy Birthday" again. The only verse the Pest joined in on was the one about looking like a monkey and smelling like one, too. She shouted the words as if she really meant them. (Dad told her to simmer down.)

Then I opened my presents. I opened Jennifer's first. She gave me a whole box full of stickers for my sticker album. A lot of the stickers were horses.

"Wow!" I cried. "Thanks, Jen!" It was a really nice gift, especially considering we'd only known each other a couple of months.

Carol gave me a cassette I'd been wanting.

And then I opened Sara's gift. It was going to be a diary. I'd saved it for last because I knew what it was and I was really excited about it. Sara and I tell each other what to give for birthdays and Christmas. That way we always get just what we want.

Only I wasn't expecting the diary to be so special. On the front was a picture of a horse that looked a lot like Peanuts. And attached to the cover was a little gold key. The key fit into a lock on the side of the diary.

"Oh, Sara, it's *beau*tiful," I breathed. "It's perfect. I've never seen anything like it." I'd been wanting a diary for a long time. I'm no great writer or any-thing, but I wanted to start keeping track of things. I wanted a record of what I was doing and what I was thinking. It would be nice to remind myself of things about Peanuts, or even of times I was mad at Katie. Like right now.

When the cake was eaten and the wrapping paper cleaned up, Sara, Carol, Jennifer and I went to my room. Mom and Dad were letting us have the port-able TV in there for the night.

I closed the door. First we spread our sleeping bags on the floor. I was going to sleep on the floor with my friends, not in bed.

Then we turned on the TV. A very spooky movie was supposed to start in ten minutes.

Jennifer shivered. "Ooh," she said, "I saw this movie last year and I was so scared I had to go to the bathroom six times while it was on."

"I had to go seven," said Carol.

"Eight," said Sara.

"Two hundred and twelve," I said. We started giggling.

We settled down on our sleeping bags and the movie began. When the first commercial came on, Carol jumped up and said, "Let's make popcorn!"

"But we'll miss the movie," said Sara.

"Oh, well, we all know what happens," I reminded her.

We made a dash for the door and thundered downstairs to the kitchen.

"Can we make popcorn?" I yelled to my mother who was in the den.

"Okay," she called back, but she sounded as if she didn't think it was a very good idea.

We made a pot of popcorn. A HUGE pot. I guess we didn't measure right. While the popcorn was popping, and we were deciding whether we wanted some more birthday cake, we heard a "bang." We saw the lid of the pot fall onto the stove, and popcorn go spilling over the side of the pot. It kept popping and popping. A mountain of popcorn was building on the stove top.

"Turn off the burner! Turn off the burner!" shrieked Sara.

Even after I turned it off we could still hear Pop! Pop! Pop-pop!

I had told Katie to stay away from my party that

night, but she came into the kitchen when she smelled the popcorn.

"Can I have some?" she asked.

"Sure, Pest," I replied. I scooped up all the popcorn that had fallen on the stove, dumped it in a bowl and handed it to her.

"But that's the dirty stuff," she cried. "Mo-om!" She went wailing into the den.

"Quick," I said. I dumped the rest of the popcorn into a large bowl and we ran upstairs with it.

We watched the movie for awhile, but for some reason it didn't seem as scary as last year.

"Let's play Truth or Dare," suggested Carol.

"Okay," I said.

Someone knocked on my door.

I opened it a crack and peeped out.

The Pest.

"Yeah?" I said.

"Phone for you."

"Really?" Maybe it was Nana and Grandpa wishing me a happy birthday. "Be right back," I said to my friends.

I went into Mom and Dad's room to pick up the phone. The Pest followed me.

"Hello?" I said. No answer. All I could hear was the dial tone.

The Pest started laughing hysterically.

I slammed the phone down. "Jerk!" I shouted. I ran back in my room and closed the door as the Pest escaped downstairs.

"Truth or dare," I said angrily to Sara.

"Dare," she answered.

"I dare you to pour water on Katie's sheets so she'll climb into a soggy, wet bed tonight."

"No," said Sara flatly.

"Yeah, come on," said Jennifer. "That's not nice."

"But she just goof-called me," I protested.

"So what?"

I glared at Sara. She glared back at me.

My glare used to make her give in, but not anymore.

"You promised," I reminded her. "You promised to help me get even."

"Only if it wasn't too mean," Sara reminded me.

"This isn't too mean. It'll be sort of funny. I'll help you, okay? I'll go with you."

"NO."

"Some friend you are," I said.

"What's that supposed to mean?"

"Who helped you when you had to be in the play last spring? Who coached you on your lines? Who stuck by you when you forgot your lines?"

Sara began to look a little pale. "That's not fair, Wendy."

"Yes, it is. It's more than fair. I helped you out for *weeks*, and all I'm asking for now is one little thing. Besides, I dared you."

"I don't know. . . ."

"Let's go," I said. I tugged at Sara's arm. She stood up reluctantly and followed me into the bathroom.

We each got a glass of water and snuck into the Pest's room. We pulled back the bedspread and blanket, and soaked her sheets with water. Then we made up the bed again.

About a half an hour later we were back in my room with Carol and Jen, telling each other our fortunes.

Suddenly we heard an "Eeeek!"

It came from the Pest's room.

Then, "Iiii-eeee! . . . Yuck . . . Mom-meee!" she called downstairs.

Mom came dashing upstairs, checked the bed, and immediately knocked on my door. "Do you know anything about Katie's bed?" she asked sternly.

None of us said anything, but our faces must have given us away.

"I'll talk to you about this tomorrow. You're in deep trouble, young lady," Mom said to me.

"But Katie started it. She was butting in on my party—and you told her not to."

"Then you're both in trouble."

"Boy," I spluttered after she'd left.

The Pest hadn't come to my party, but she'd managed to ruin it anyway. What a jerk.

8.

A Home for Peanuts

Tuesday, August 1
Today was the worst day in my
whole, entire life. I'm so sad
I don't know what to do. I can't
ever ride Peanuts again. Ever.

That was the third entry in my new diary. There wasn't much space for each day, or I would have written more. I had a lot to say. I was sorry I had to put something so awful near the beginning of such a nice diary, but what could I do? That was the truth about Peanuts. The rotten truth. I'd never ride her again. No one would.

The horrible day had actually gotten off to a good start. Katie had decided she needed to practice the piano that afternoon. She had another summer recital coming up and she was going to play a very difficult piece. It was so difficult she'd have to miss riding lessons to practice it. Also, she had a cold. So I got to go to Hasty Acres without her tagging along.

I hopped on the bus feeling as happy as a lark. I had turned ten years old, I was wearing my fancy green hat, and the Pest was at home. Mandy and I sang songs all the way to Hasty Acres.

When we got there I ran for Peanuts's stall. I rode her at every lesson now. She'd become "my" horse, just the way Daybreak had become Mandy's and Eugene had become Vicky's. Today I had two sugar cubes and an apple slice for Peanuts. I had even peeled the apple, in case she didn't like skin.

"Hi!" I greeted Chris as I ran through the stable yard and into the stable.

"Hi," he called. "Hey. . . . Wendy?"

"I'll be right there," I shouted over my shoulder. It had only been five days since I'd seen Peanuts, but it felt like five months.

Behind me I could hear Chris saying something else, but I didn't stop to find out what.

I ran by Sky High's stall and he snorted rudely at me.

I ran by Daybreak's stall and saw him rolling in the wood chips.

I ran by Mr. Chips's stall, stopped, went back, and patted him quickly on the nose. (Mr. Chips was my second favorite horse.)

Then I continued on my way to Peanuts's stall.

But when I got there, it was empty. "Hey, who beat me to Peanuts?" I said aloud.

Boy, was that unfair. Now that we had claimed horses of our own, nobody else ever took them. I turned and glared at Chris in the stable yard. But he didn't see me. He was talking to Paula.

Where *was* Peanuts, anyway? She wasn't saddled up with Chris.

I looked in her stall once more to make absolutely sure it was empty. Then I started walking back out. I met Paula halfway.

"Hey," I said accusingly, "who got Peanuts? Do we have a new student?"

Paula shook her head. "Listen, Wendy, I want to talk to you. Let's go in the office."

The "office" was really the tack room, where the saddles and other riding equipment were kept. There were two chairs, a falling-apart sofa, and a rickety desk where Mrs. Larrick worked.

Paula sat on the sofa and motioned me to sit next to her. She looked very serious, and I began to feel nervous. Had I done something wrong? Were they kicking me out because they'd found out I'd told the

Pest to ride Sky High her first day?

"Wendy," Paula began, "I know how much Peanuts means to you. I know she's your favorite horse, and that you feel most comfortable riding her . . ."

I nodded. "Your mother said we make a good team."

"That's right. I also know that you're one of the most skilled riders in your class, and that you can learn to ride any horse well."

"Thanks . . ." I said uncertainly.

Paula paused. Finally she said in a rush, "I guess there's no easy way to tell you this. Peanuts got hurt yesterday, Wendy. I was riding her in the woods. We jumped over a low fence and there was a chuckhole on the other side. Peanuts came down in it and injured her leg. She's going to be okay, but she can't be ridden again. She was getting old anyway."

"Can't be ridden?" I repeated numbly. "Where is she?"

"We've got her fixed up in a smaller stall in one of the barns. We need to keep her in a place where she can't move around much. She has to stay quiet."

"How long until she gets better?" I asked. I could feel tears starting. I thought maybe if I kept talking I wouldn't cry.

"A few weeks, probably."

"And then what? What do you do with a horse you can't ride?"

"Oh, Wendy, don't worry. Nothing horrible." Paula smiled.

"Will you keep her here?"

"Probably not. We can't afford to keep a horse we can't use in the lessons. But we'll find a good home for her. We'll find someone who will take her as a pet. She can spend all her time lazing around in some big field, and pretend she's gone into retirement."

I tried to laugh, but it came out more as a sob. Then I began to cry, and Paula put her arms around me and held me. After awhile she handed me a tissue and said, "Come on. Dry your eyes. Your lesson has started and Mom needs us. Chris saved Mr. Chips for you. He's saddled and ready to go."

I stood shakily. I hardly knew what I was doing. No more Peanuts, I told myself. No more Peanuts. It was so terrible that I don't think all the terribleness had sunk in yet.

It was while I was trotting around the ring on Mr. Chips that it hit me. As soon as the Larricks found a home for Peanuts, I'd probably never see her again. She'd go off to some other farm. It could be miles away. It could be clear across the country.

I steered Mr. Chips to the side of the ring and let the other kids ride by me. I wondered if they knew about Peanuts. I wondered if they could tell I was crying.

"Wendy?" asked Paula. She was standing next to Mr. Chips, holding his bridle.

"Could I see Peanuts, please?" I asked, wiping my eyes.

"Wendy, I don't think that's a very good idea."

"*Please?* It's almost the end of the lesson. I just want to *see* her."

"Well . . . all right."

Paula ran over to speak to her mother. Then she and I walked Mr. Chips back to the stables and gave him to Chris.

"This way," said Paula. She led me behind the stables, across a gravelly yard, and into a small wooden barn next to a toolshed.

We waited for our eyes to adjust to the darkness. After a few seconds, Paula walked toward one of the stalls. She began talking softly. "Okay, Peanuts. Hi there, Peanuts."

I followed Paula. I could see Peanuts standing in the stall. I stood on my tiptoes and peeped over the door. On her right front leg was a fat bandage.

Peanuts looked at us, but she didn't move. She

just stood there. I glanced at Paula. This wasn't the Peanuts I knew.

"She's really all right," Paula told me. "Just worn out."

"Oh, Peanuts," was all I could say.

Finally Peanuts blinked her dark eyes and let out a soft whuffle.

I stroked her neck.

"Well, good-bye," I said at last. "We have to go now."

We left the barn.

"Can I see Peanuts again on Thursday?" I asked. "She'll still be here, won't she?"

"Oh, I'm sure she'll be here for awhile," replied Paula. "We're not going to move her until she's all well. You can visit her on Thursday. Sure."

"Thanks, Paula."

Paula gave my hand a squeeze. I smiled at her. But all the way home on the bus I stared out the window and thought of Peanuts.

At dinner that night I told everyone what had happened. Katie was mad that she had missed out on the excitement. She would be. I was very glad she hadn't been there to see me cry.

The Pest wanted to know every detail. "What did Peanuts look like?" she asked. "Was her leg swollen?

Was the bandage bloody? How did Paula get her home after the accident? Did the veterinarian give her a shot?"

I ignored her. "You know what the worst thing is?"

Mom and Dad shook their heads.

"What?" asked Scottie.

"No one can ride her anymore. So the Larricks are giving her away."

Katie's eyes grew wide.

"Oh, honey," said Mom. "I'm sorry. I know how much you like Peanuts."

"Yeah. They're going to find someone who wants her just for a pet."

"I'm sure they'll find a good home for her, lamb," said Dad. "You don't have to worry about that."

"Oh, I'm not worried."

"You're not?"

"No. See, I think I know someone who would give her a good home."

"Who?" asked Mom.

"Me! Please, please, please, Mom? Dad? She could use our backyard for a pasture. We could—"

"Wendy, I don't think so," my mother said.

"*Please?* Our backyard is huge."

"N-O."

Then the Pest spoke up. "Peanuts could help us

save money," she said. She glanced at me.

"Yeah?" I asked.

"She could graze on our lawn. We wouldn't need the gardeners to come mow it anymore."

"Katie—" Dad started to say.

"And we wouldn't waste food. She could eat our table scraps."

Mom and Dad smiled at each other.

"That's a nice thought, lamb," Dad said to Katie. Then he looked at me. "If you really want a horse, maybe we could think about getting one and boarding it out at Hasty Acres."

I nodded my head. But that wasn't exactly what I'd meant. We'd have to pay to board a horse, and Mom and Dad would probably want me to help earn some of the money. But how could I ever earn enough? Besides, I wanted Peanuts—here with me. What was the point of keeping her at Hasty Acres when I couldn't ride her? I'd have to go all the way out there just to look at her. No doubt about it, our backyard would be much more convenient.

Later that evening, the Pest poked her head in my room.

I was lying on my bed, finishing up *Brighty of the Grand Canyon*.

"What are you doing?" asked the Pest.

"What's it look like?" I replied.

The Pest didn't answer. She stepped into my room and handed me a piece of paper.

"What's this?"

"Read it," said the Pest.

I looked at the paper. It was a list. Across the top, it said:

WHY WE SHOULD KEEP PEANUTS

Under that, the Pest had written:

1. We've never had a pet and we really want one.
2. Peanuts needs a home.
3. Peanuts would keep our mowing bills down.
4. Scottie likes ponies.
5. *Wendy needs Peanuts and Peanuts needs Wendy.*

I put the paper down and looked at Katie. "This is pretty good," I told her.

"Yeah?"

"Mm-hmmm." I frowned.

"When should we show it to Mommy and Daddy?"

"I don't know," I answered. "Maybe we should wait awhile."

"All right. Do you want to add anything to it?"

I thought a minute. I wasn't very good at this kind

of thing. "Not now," I said. "But we won't show it to Mom and Dad until tomorrow night. We can add to it till then."

"Okay." Katie left the list with me and went back to her room.

The next morning, Sara and Carol and I met in Carol's tree fort. I told them about Peanuts and showed them Katie's list.

"This is a good list," said Carol.

"Yeah," agreed Sara.

"We can add to it," I told them.

"Hmm," said Carol. "Put down *Horses prevent heart attacks*."

"*What?* Come on, Carol. This is serious."

"I'm *being* serious. I heard this guy on TV. This doctor. He was saying how pets calm people down. And so I was thinking, since heart attacks can be caused by stress, then pets probably help prevent heart attacks."

"Well . . . okay," I said. I wrote: *6. Horses help prevent heart attacks*. "Sara? Anything?" I asked.

Sara gazed out of the tree fort. "How about: *Pets teach responsibility?*"

"Oh, great!" I jotted that down, too.

We thought some more and I added: *8. Horses are good company*, before we put the list away.

"Have you decided how to get even with Katie?" Sara asked me.

"Not yet," I replied. "But now I have a lot to get even with her for. After my party, Mom and Dad said we couldn't watch TV for a whole week."

"She just made you this list, though," protested Carol.

"So? She horned in on my riding lessons, and I still have four more days to go without television."

"Didn't Katie get punished, too?"

"Yeah, but neither of us would have gotten punished at all if she hadn't played that trick on me."

Carol and Sara were silent.

"Some friends *you* guys are!" I said, and stomped down the tree fort ladder.

"Wendy," Sara called after me, but I ignored her.

Ten minutes later we made up. Miss J. had baked a big batch of carob health cookies, so I carried a tray with a pitcher of juice and a plate of cookies to the tree fort. Carol and Sara and I had a snack and apologized to each other.

But as far as I was concerned, I had one more thing to get even with Katie for.

I decided to show the list to Mom and Dad right after dinner. Katie came with me. I didn't want her to, but the list was half hers.

Mom and Dad read the piece of paper carefully. Then they looked up and Mom said, "Girls, this is a very thoughtful list. But for every reason you've included here, Dad and I have a reason for *not* taking Peanuts."

"Like what?" I demanded.

"Well," said Dad, "number one, horses need more space than we have here. Two, the upkeep of a horse is expensive. Three, we don't have a stall . . . and we can't use the garage," he added quickly when he saw me open my mouth. "We will not leave the cars out in the cold all winter because a horse is living in the garage. Four, we don't have a horse van to transport Peanuts. And—"

"All *right*," I butted in.

"But Daddy," Katie spoke up. "We want a pet."

"We understand," said Mom. "But Peanuts is not the pet for us. Nor is any other horse. Wouldn't you like something smaller? A goldfish, maybe?"

"Fish are stupid pets," I said.

"I'm sorry," said Dad. "No Peanuts. *No horse*. Now go get ready for bed."

The next day was Thursday. In the morning, the Pest was in another piano recital at her music school. Guess what. She won first place in Class IV again.

So what else is new?

9.

Ways to Keep Peanuts

"Hi, Peanuts," I said softly.

It was Thursday afternoon and I was at Hasty Acres. Paula had told me I could visit Peanuts before the lesson began.

"How are you doing?"

Peanuts looked a lot better. At least, she seemed glad to see me. As soon as I had entered the barn, she'd thrust her head over the stall door. Now she was smacking her lips. I knew she wanted a treat. I was prepared.

I held out a piece of carrot. She took it gently and crunched away while I patted her nose.

"Good girl. Are you feeling better?" I asked her.

Crunch, crunch. Crunch, crunch.

When she finished, I gave her a sugar cube for dessert.

I looked at my watch. I had to leave. Peanuts blinked her eyes and watched me go out the door.

Chris had saddled Mr. Chips for me. During the lesson we trotted around and around the ring. I was pretty good at posting now.

So was Katie. I couldn't believe it. She wasn't as good as I was—she'd lose the rhythm every now and then—but she was one of the better ones in our class. Twice today, Mrs. Larrick had called out, "Good work, Katie!" and Katie had beamed. Then she had looked over her shoulder at me triumphantly.

Katie still needed to work on control, though. That seemed to be hardest for her. She could mount and dismount, walk and trot, but when it came to being firm with her horse, she lost something. Maybe because she really was a little afraid of horses. She hadn't gotten over that.

"Class, please dismount," said Mrs. Larrick after awhile. It was only ten minutes to four. Usually we didn't dismount until exactly four o'clock.

We lined our horses up across the middle of the ring and dismounted.

"I have an announcement to make," said Mrs. Larrick. "Every year at the end of the summer we hold a horse show at Hasty Acres."

My heart gave a little leap. A horse show!

"Anyone who's taking lessons here can be in the show, from beginners to the most advanced students. If you prefer not to take part, that's fine, but I suggest you give it a try. It's lots of fun, and it will be a good experience, especially if you plan to continue riding."

Mrs. Larrick glanced at me. If she was wondering whether I'd be in the show, she could quit worrying. This was what I'd been waiting for all summer! I hoped there would be prizes.

"The show will be held in about a month," continued Mrs. Larrick, "on September second, the Saturday after the summer session ends. You will show with your class, and we'll prepare together during the next few weeks, but you will be judged individually. And prizes will be awarded to individuals. In other words, this class will show as a group, but you'll be competing against each other."

Her last few words cut through me like an icy knife. Up until I heard them, I'd been feeling pretty confident. Here was my chance to win a prize. But "competing against each other" meant competing against Katie. How could I beat out the Prize Queen? The Pest always won prizes; I never did.

And wasn't Mrs. Larrick always saying, "Good

work, Katie," and "Nice form, Katie," and "Very good, Katie"? If Katie was so good now, how good would she be in a month? As good as I was? . . . Better than I was?

I shuddered. If I was in a contest with the Pest and she won and I lost, it would be worse than watching her win any of her other awards. It would be horrible.

"Please let me know as soon as possible whether you'll be in the show," Mrs. Larrick was saying. "It'll be sponsored by Red Rose Feeds—that's the company we buy our horse feed from—and we have to let them know ahead of time how many will be participating. All right?"

We nodded.

"Okay, lead your horses back to the stables."

I tried to feel excited about the show . . . but I was too worried.

As soon as the Pest and I got home after the lesson, I changed out of my riding clothes and called Sara on the phone. I closed the door to Mom and Dad's room and lay on the floor with my feet propped up on their bed.

"Guess what," I said, as soon as Sara answered the phone.

"What." She knew it was me.

"I'm going to be in a horse show."

"Oh, Wendy, that's great! I know you'll win a prize. . . . There will be prizes, won't there?"

"Sure," I said.

"Well, you'll win one."

"I hope so." I didn't say anything about the Pest. I didn't feel like talking about her.

"I know so."

"What are you doing now?" I asked.

"Nothing. What are you doing?"

"Nothing."

"Want to come over?" asked Sara.

"Okay. I'll be right there."

" 'Bye."

" 'Bye."

" 'Bye."

"I said 'bye."

"You hang up first."

"No, you."

"No, you."

"I can't."

"Wait. Count to three."

"One . . . two . . . three," we said together. We hung up at the exact same moment.

I raced over to Sara's.

"Let's *do* something," she said when I got there. She was sitting on her back stoop. "I'm tired of reading and tired of knitting and tired of drawing and I'm even tired of Star and Lucy. . . . No offense," she said to Star, as he came trotting around a corner of the house. "The summer's getting boring."

"You say that at the beginning of every August," I reminded her.

"I know."

"And then by the last day of summer vacation you're moping around, saying how can you face another nine and a half months of school, and why did you waste so much of the summer."

"I know," Sara said again.

We sat with our chins in our hands and our elbows propped on our knees.

"Hey, I've got an idea!" I cried suddenly.

"What?" asked Sara, a glimmer of excitement in her eyes.

"Let's think up ways to get Peanuts," I answered.

"Yeah," said Sara slowly.

"I know! We could kidnap her!" I suggested.

"How?" whispered Sara.

"Okay. We sneak over to Hasty Acres in the middle of the night, open the door to Peanuts's stall— I know right where it is—and lead her out. She'll come with us. She knows me."

"Yeah," said Sara, "then what?"

"Then we sneak her back home and hide her in the garage."

"Yeah!"

"Oh, but wait. Hasty Acres is at least four miles from here, and we can't walk that far."

"Neither can Peanuts," pointed out Sara.

"And we couldn't really hide her in the garage," I added.

Sara shook her head.

We thought some more.

"You could buy her," said Sara after awhile.

"Buy her what?" I asked.

"No, I mean *buy* her. Pay for her. Save up enough money. How much do you think a horse would cost? An *old* horse?"

"I'm not sure. Fifty dollars?"

"That's a lot. How much have you got?"

"Six dollars and ten cents. And Carol owes me a quarter."

"Nowhere near enough."

After that, we didn't have any more ideas.

"At least I'm going away this weekend," Sara said finally.

"You are?"

"Yeah. Mom and Dad and me and Uncle John and Aunt Martha and Carol. We're going to Barnegat Bay for three whole days."

Sara and Carol and their families take a vacation together every year. I wished I were going with them. Now I'd be stuck with a long, boring weekend.

On Saturday morning, Dad went to the nursery to buy shrubs. Mom took Scottie to the dentist. And Miss J. had the day off.

I sat at the kitchen table and looked across the breakfast dishes at the Pest.

She smiled at me.

"What are you going to do today?" I asked her. I figured the Pest would have a hundred good answers. She could write a book. She could paint a masterpiece. She could compose a sonata. She could invent something and get her picture in the paper again.

"I don't know," she replied. "What are you going to do?"

I shrugged.

The Pest poured herself another bowl of Grape Nuts.

"Don't you have to practice?" I asked her.

"Nope. Not unless I want to."

I got up and began putting dishes in the sink.

"Wendy," said the Pest, "do you think Mommy and Daddy really meant it when they said we couldn't keep Peanuts?"

"Yeah. Why? Don't you?"

The Pest crunched thoughtfully on a mouthful of cereal. She swallowed. "I'm not sure. If we could just come up with a good enough plan . . ."

"Like what?"

"I don't know. Let's think."

"I've thought," I said.

"Well, what if we could make Mommy and Daddy think they *needed* a horse?"

"Yeah . . ."

"Why do people get horses in the first place?"

"Because they love them?"

Katie frowned and crunched away at her Grape Nuts. "Nah. You could love mice or snakes or cats just as easily. What do you need *horses* for?"

"To pull wagons?"

"That's what I mean!" cried Katie. "What else?"

"To go places where cars can't go!"

"To get you through the snow and ice!" added Katie.

"Oh, but wait," I said. "We can't ride Peanuts. And I bet she can't pull anything."

Katie's face fell. "You're right," she said sadly.

"Katie," I ventured, "you really want to help me get Peanuts, don't you?"

Katie nodded.

"Why?" I asked.

"Because *you* want her."

I considered that. I remembered her private conversation with Mom. She was trying to be my friend.

"Thanks," I said at last.

That evening I opened my diary to August 5th and wrote:

> Katie wants to help me keep Peanuts. She's
> being very nice. Maybe the Pest is getting
> less pesty.

I snapped the diary closed. And that was when I realized I hadn't had to unlock it to write in it. Someone had broken the lock. And there were faint smudges on the white cover and on some of the pages. I knew Mom and Dad and Miss J. wouldn't read my diary. And Scottie *couldn't* read yet.

That left the Pest.

Angrily I flipped through the pages, scrunching a few by accident. Then I wasted all of the space for August 6th and part of the space for August 7th writing:

I TAKE IT BACK. KATIE IS A *GIGANTIC* PEST AFTER ALL. SHE IS A SNEAK. AND BY THE WAY, I WONDER IF SHE KNOWS THAT THE DENTIST TOLD MOM AND DAD HER TEETH ARE SO UGLY SHE'LL HAVE TO WEAR BRACES FROM THE TIME SHE'S TEN UNTIL SHE'S TWENTY-NINE.

There. That would teach her.

I didn't even bother to hide the diary. I hoped the Pest would sneak in and read it again.

10.

Getting Even

The Pest spent all day Sunday hiding her mouth behind her hands and smiling with her lips pressed together. She did more hiding than smiling. You could tell she was pretty nervous.

Mom and Dad knew something was bothering her. They didn't want to press the Pest, though. They tried to ignore her behavior. But when she began talking with her lips closed Dad finally asked gently, "Is anything wrong, lamb?"

The Pest shook her head and said, "Mmphhmmnfll."

"Katie, I can't understand you. What's wrong with your mouth?"

"*You* know!" The Pest finally exploded. She risked opening her mouth.

"I do?" asked Dad.

"About my teeth," said the Pest. She was ready to burst into tears.

"Your teeth . . . ?"

"How they're so ugly I'm going to need braces for nineteen years."

I couldn't help it. I started giggling. I did it as quietly as I could, but Dad heard me anyway. He looked at me sharply.

"Wendy? Do you know something about this?"

I tried to stop laughing. "Ask the P–, ask Katie where she got the idea."

The Pest turned on me. Her eyes were daggers.

"Go ahead. Tell Dad," I said.

"Flmnphhrmlnstp."

"*What?*" Dad was losing his patience.

"From Wendy's diary," the Pest mumbled.

"You were reading Wendy's diary?"

The Pest nodded.

"Did Wendy say you could?"

The Pest shook her head miserably. She'd been caught red-handed.

"Up to your room, Katie, while I talk to your mother."

I walked off, smirking, while the Pest headed for her room.

* * *

Mom and Dad told the Pest she'd have to spend the rest of the day (except for dinner) in her room, and go to bed an hour early.

Around four o'clock I crept upstairs and peeped in her room. Katie was kneeling on her bed gazing sulkily out the window. I knew she was watching Scottie play in the sprinkler and wishing she were out there with him.

"It's too bad about your punishment," I said.

The Pest whirled around. "Shut up, Wendy!"

"I mean, really. First a week with no TV and now this. It's a shame."

"Shut up. Just shut up!"

And then an idea came to me. A mean one. A *really* mean one. A way to get even with Katie. It was the perfect plan—and Sara wasn't here to help me. Oh, well. I was certain it was too mean an idea to interest her anyway.

"You know," I told Katie, stepping into her room, "you could run away."

The Pest forgot to be angry with me. She opened her eyes wide. "I *could?*" she squeaked.

"Mmm hmm. It would sure show Mom and Dad."

"Yeah . . ." the Pest said thoughtfully.

"If you ran away, they'd see how horrible they'd been to you."

"Yeah . . ." The Pest began to look excited.

"They'd really miss you."

"Yeah . . ."

"But maybe it's not such a good idea," I added.

"Yes, it is! Yes, it is!" cried the Pest. She was all worked up.

"You'll worry Mom and Dad."

"I know."

"They'll feel terrible."

"I *know*," said the Pest dreamily.

"Are you going to do it?" I asked. I was already sure she would.

"Yes. I am. I really, really am."

"Well, don't say I didn't warn you."

"Okay."

"Remember, I said this was a bad idea. I said you'll worry Mom and Dad."

"Okay, okay." The Pest was barely listening. She was flying around her room, opening drawers, tossing things out. "Wendy, could you get my suitcase out of the attic?" she asked.

"Oh, goodness, Katie. You want me to *help* you? I better not. I don't want to get in any trouble."

"I won't tell. I promise," said the Pest breathlessly. She opened the door to her closet and pulled out a jacket and two pairs of running shoes. "*Please*, Wendy? Come on."

"All right. But I know this is wrong," I muttered.

I smiled to myself as I rummaged around in the attic, but by the time I handed Katie her suitcase, I looked very serious. I even managed to work up a few tears.

"Here," I sniffled. "I'm really going to miss you." I wiped my eyes with the back of my hand.

"Thanks," said Katie, busily stuffing things in the suitcase. In a few minutes it was so full we had to sit on it to close it.

"Hey!" whispered Katie. "Shh! I think someone's coming. Check the hallway."

I did. No one was there.

"It's your imagination," I told her.

The Pest hauled her suitcase over to the doorway. She turned and looked around her room. "Well, good-bye, room," she said softly. "Good-bye, bed. Good-bye, dresser. Good-bye, Mr. Mumps." (Mr. Mumps was her stuffed monkey. We couldn't fit him in the suitcase.) "Good-bye, clock. Good-bye, doll carriage."

Katie's good-byes went on for quite awhile. What a jerk.

Finally she closed the door to her room. "Mommy and Daddy will think I'm in there! They'll think the door is shut because I'm mad!" she said gleefully.

"Now listen, Wendy. Don't tell them anything. Pretend you don't know what I did. They probably won't miss me until dinner."

"Oh, boy. You're going to get me in—"

"No, I won't. I'll take all the blame."

Perfect. Just what I wanted to hear.

"Hey, where are you going to go?" I asked suddenly.

"Oh, I don't know. I'll think of something."

The Pest made me go downstairs and find out where Mom and Dad were. When I gave her the all-clear signal, she tiptoed after me and snuck out the back door.

I watched her disappear into the woods behind our house. I knew that if she went far enough, she'd wind up at the playground in back of our school. Sometimes we used the woods as a shortcut to or from school. But there was no path, and Mom and Dad didn't really like us in the woods alone. They said you never knew.

After the Pest left, I sat on our back porch. I was dying to tell someone my secret, but there was no one to tell. When Miss J. finally announced that dinner was ready, I shot out of my chair. My heart was pounding. I went to the kitchen to wash my hands. Mom was there, telling Scottie to go upstairs and get Katie.

In a few minutes he came running back downstairs.

"Mommy!" he cried. "I knocked and knocked on Katie's door but there was no answer, so I went in and she's *gone!*"

Mom and Dad looked at each other. Then they tore upstairs. I followed them.

"Wow," I said, peering around Katie's room at the open dresser drawers and the empty coat hangers in the closet. "I bet she ran away."

"Oh, *no*," my mother moaned.

"Now, calm down, everyone," said Dad. "I'm sure she's fine. She'll be back soon."

"I don't know," said Mom. "Maybe we should call the police."

The police! I hadn't counted on that.

"Does anyone know how long she's been gone?" asked Dad.

"The last time I saw her was around four-thirty," I replied.

"Why, that's two *hours* ago!" cried Mom.

"Honey, she's probably not very far away. She could even be hiding in the house. For all we know, she can hear this conversation," said Dad. "Let's look for her ourselves before we call the police."

I felt a little funny helping Mom and Dad and Miss J. and Scottie search our house for the Pest when I knew we wouldn't find her. After about ten minutes, I said, "Maybe she's outside. I'm going to check the yard."

"Me, too," said Scottie.

"And you and I can look in the woods," Mom said to Dad.

"I'll stay in the house in case she comes home by herself," suggested Miss J.

So we split up. But after pretending to search the yard for a while, I began to feel sort of sorry for myself. I was starving because we hadn't eaten dinner. I had a headache, and on top of everything else, I had expected Mom and Dad to be angry with the Pest. They didn't seem angry at all.

"I found her! I found her!" Mom suddenly shouted.

A few seconds later, Mom and Dad and Katie came out of the woods. Dad was carrying the suitcase. The Pest was crying. She had fallen down and skinned her knees. She'd been chased by a dog. Two big boys had teased her. And she'd lost her fake diamond ring.

For awhile, Katie got a ton of attention—a bubble bath and supper in bed.

I fumed.

But the evening wasn't a total loss. After Mom and Dad and the Pest had a long talk, they said no more TV for another week, *and* no allowance for two weeks.

And the Pest never said a word about me.

11.

August

By Tuesday, the Pest had gotten over Sunday. Sort of. We went off to Hasty Acres with notes that said we could be in the show on September second. We didn't speak much, but that was okay with me. I was busy thinking about something else. I had another note with me. This one was for Paula and it said I wanted to take a few private lessons before the show.

That had been my idea. I remembered Paula's offer. The one she had made way back before my birthday and before Peanuts got hurt. Well, now I had a good reason to want some extra help. I was determined to win a prize in the show. Nothing was going to stop me. Not even Katie. I was a good rider, but I had to be better. (Katie had asked for

private lessons, too, but Mom and Dad said absolutely not. Her schedule was too busy already. And
Katie hadn't argued. I don't think she'd really wanted
the lessons. She just wanted to copy me.)

When our lesson was over, Mrs. Larrick collected
our notes. Everybody in our group was going to be
in the show except Tom. His family would be away
that weekend.

Then I gave Paula the other note.

"What's this?" she asked.

"It's from my mother and father. I want to take
some private lessons. Before the show. You said I
could, remember?"

"Sure I do. That's great, Wendy. Can you come
out here on Saturdays?"

"I think so," I said. "I'll have to check, but I think
that's okay."

It was okay. Mom and Dad said I could have
private lessons on the three Saturdays before the
show. And that was how August got to be the busiest
month of my life.

On Saturdays, Paula and I would spend about an
hour in the ring, and then another half hour or so
riding in the fields. In the fields, Mr. Chips could
trot to his heart's content, and I really got the feel
of posting. Sometimes he would break into a canter,

which scared me, but I knew how to slow him down.

Mr. Chips was the horse I was going to ride in the Hasty Acres horse show. After Peanuts had been injured, I'd started riding him. When Mrs. Larrick asked us to choose the horse we would compete with, I was the first one to raise my hand and tell her my decision.

I began jogging in the mornings. Paula said it was important to stay in shape. She didn't tell me to jog, but Mom and Dad usually went jogging before breakfast. I decided that joining them was as good a way as any to stay in shape. Also, I went over to Jennifer's house and swam laps in her pool a few times.

I was feeling very good about myself, and very good about my riding. "Wendy," Paula told me on the second Saturday lesson, "I hope you're going to keep coming to Hasty Acres. I think you could skip the advanced beginners' class and join the inter-mediates this fall."

"All right!" I cried.

"And something else. Chris has been complaining lately. He says he needs help. We're looking for someone to give him a hand mucking out stalls and grooming the horses. Would you like an after-school job? You could learn a lot."

"Would I? Oh, *yes!*" I threw my arms around

Paula, and then planted a huge kiss on Mr. Chips's nose. He looked startled at first, but the next thing I knew he was whuffling in my ear. Just the way Peanuts used to do.

A few days later, Katie and I went to our next to last Tuesday riding class. The Pest had a particularly good lesson, from start to finish. She mounted Daffodil easily.

"Excellent, Katie!" said Mrs. Larrick.

We walked around the ring.

We trotted around the ring.

I kept watching the Pest.

She took her turn trotting alone.

"Nice!" called Mrs. Larrick.

But when Katie reached the end of the line, she didn't stop Daffodil *quite* soon enough. And she wouldn't pull his head away when he nibbled at Daybreak's hoof long enough to make Daybreak look like he might kick Daffodil.

After that, though, the Pest was great.

And I was worried.

I knew I was a very good rider. I kept thinking about everything I was learning with Paula, and about skipping into the intermediate class.

But I was still worried.

No question about it. Katie had improved. She was a good rider, too.

It was after this lesson that Paula pulled me aside and said, "Can you come out on Saturday about half an hour earlier than usual?"

"I guess so," I replied. "Why?"

But before Paula could answer, the Pest tripped over a rock, skinned her elbow, and bit her lip.

We had to find the first-aid kit, and Mrs. Larrick thought the Pest might even need stitches in her lip. But her lip stopped bleeding after a few minutes and we got her bandaged up and loaded on the bus. I didn't remember about going to Hasty Acres early until we were halfway home.

On Saturday, Dad drove me to my lesson. I got there twenty-five minutes early. I would have been a whole half an hour early except that before we left, the Pest was sure she had lost her piano book in Dad's car. She made us look under the seats and in the glove compartment and everywhere before she found it inside the piano bench.

Dad dropped me off in front of the farmhouse. The first thing I saw was Paula striding over to me. The next thing I saw was a horse van.

"Hi, Paula! Are you taking one of the horses to a

show?" I asked. I shut the car door and waved to Dad as he turned the car around and drove away.

Paula shook her head. "No. This is why I wanted you to come early. The van is for Peanuts. She's well enough to be moved, and we've found a home for her."

"You have?" I gulped.

"A very nice family—the Fords. They have three children and a big farm with plenty of room for Peanuts. The kids are glad to have another pet to take care of. They love horses and don't mind that they can't ride Peanuts. And they live just three miles from here."

"Oh," I said.

"I thought you might want to say good-bye to Peanuts."

I nodded. I could feel a lump in my throat.

"Come on," said Paula. She took my hand.

We walked to the stable where Peanuts had been moved back to her stall several days ago. Paula let me go in alone.

I noticed that Peanuts's nameplate had been taken down. I wondered if it would go with her to her new home. I wondered what name would go up in its place.

Peanuts was in her stall, still wearing the bandage on her leg. She was moving around restlessly. She

knew something was going on. People had been bus-
tling in and out of her stall all morning, Paula said.

"Peanuts," I called.

She jerked her head up.

"Hi, there." I tried to swallow that lump in my
throat.

Peanuts rolled her eyes. She looked a bit wild.

"Here," I said. I pulled a sugar cube from my
pocket and held it toward her.

She shook her head, her mane and forelock swish-
ing, and stumbled away from me.

"Peanuts? Come here. Calm down. It's okay. You
remember me, don't you? . . . Don't you?"

She came close enough for me to pat her nose.
That calmed her down a little. I tried the sugar cube
again. This time she took it quickly. But she re-
treated a few steps to eat it. When she finished, she
stayed where she was.

"Aren't you going to come back?" I asked. "Come
on. I want to kiss you good-bye. That's all."

"Wendy!" Paula called from outside. "Mom and
I are coming in now."

"No!" I cried. "Just a—"

"I'm sorry. Mr. Ford is waiting," said Mrs. Larrick.

She and Paula came in and led Peanuts from her
stall.

"Is she okay?" I asked Paula tearfully.

"She's nervous," Paula replied. "She senses something, a change. But she'll adjust."

I watched as Mrs. Larrick and Mr. Ford coaxed her up a ramp into the van and closed the door.

"Good-bye, Peanuts," I whispered as the van rattled down the driveway.

"Hey," said Paula, coming over to stand next to me. "I'm sorry. Maybe I shouldn't have asked you to come out for this."

I looked at Paula, who was brushing tears from her eyes.

"That's okay," I said. "I'm glad I got to say good-bye."

Paula nodded.

"Maybe we could go see Peanuts at the Fords's farm sometime?" I suggested.

"Sure."

Paula and I looked at each other.

"Well, come on, kiddo," she said finally. "You've got some work to do. There's just one week until the show."

One week! Was I really good enough to win a prize? Good enough not to be beaten by Katie?

I mounted Mr. Chips and worked out harder than ever.

12.

Hasty Acres Horse Show

The heat wave began the day after my last private lesson. On Monday, the temperature rose to ninety-five degrees. It stayed around there until Thursday, when it crept up to ninety-eight degrees. When I woke up on Saturday, the morning of the horse show, it was already ninety-one degrees. Ninety-one degrees at seven o'clock. Yech. I had dripped and perspired my way through the Tuesday and Thursday lessons. I hoped I wouldn't look too horrible in the show.

I rolled out of bed and stumbled over to the mirror. I had butterflies in my stomach. There must have been an awful lot of them in there. My stomach was jumping all over the place.

I took a couple of deep breaths and tried to calm

down. "You don't have a thing to worry about," I told myself. "You've been practicing hard with Mr. Chips. You and Mr. Chips are almost as good a team as you and Peanuts were."

Katie crept into my thoughts.

"And you do *not* need to worry about the Pest," I scolded myself. "Even if she is the Prize Queen. You'd better concentrate on yourself and forget about her."

I brushed my hair until it shone, then pulled it into two ponytails. My hair was really too short for ponytails, so a lot escaped at the sides and down the back of my neck. I decided to ignore it. It was going to be too hot to leave my hair loose.

I found two red ribbons and tied them around the ponytails. There. That looked better.

I put on a T-shirt and a pair of shorts. I'd put on the riding outfit later.

I went downstairs to the kitchen.

"Morning, lamb," Dad greeted me.

He and Mom had just gotten back from jogging. I'd decided not to go with them. I wanted to save all my energy for the show.

"Morning," I said.

"It's going to be hot again today, honey," said Mom. "Maybe over a hundred degrees. Dress as coolly as you can, okay?"

"Okay. Gosh, why does it have to be a hundred degrees for the show? We're going to look *awful*. We'll sweat and the horses will sweat and the dust will stick all over us. I bet a lot of people won't even come, because it'll be so hot."

"Well, *we'll* be there," Mom assured me with a smile.

Right. What was I complaining about anyway? This was my big chance to win a prize. I had to stop thinking about the weather and Katie and start concentrating on the show.

At ten o'clock, the thermometer on the back porch read ninety-six degrees.

Mom, Dad, Miss J., Scottie, the Pest, and I piled into Dad's car and backed down the driveway. Waiting by our mailbox were Carol and Sara. They tumbled into the back of the station wagon with me.

"I'm so glad you could come!" I exclaimed.

"Oh, we wouldn't miss it. I want to see you win a prize," said Sara.

I poked her. "Shh," I warned.

But nobody had heard. I hoped.

The Pest was in the front seat between Mom and Dad, complaining about the heat, and wanting to know why we didn't have an air-conditioned car. In the backseat, Miss J. was showing Scottie all the stuff she'd brought along in case he got bored.

I leaned against the window and tried to relax. Those butterflies were fluttering up a storm. I hadn't even been this nervous when I'd had one of the biggest parts in the play last spring.

"*Calm down,*" I told myself sharply. "You'll be riding Mr. Chips, and Mrs. Larrick says you're a good rider. It'll be okay."

The driveway to Hasty Acres looked like a freeway. I guess the heat wasn't keeping people from the show after all. There were cars backed up from the road to the farmhouse. We crept along until we reached the end of the drive. Charlie was there directing traffic. He motioned us into a wide field where Dad parked the car.

We got out and followed a stream of people to the grassy field where the riding rings were. Then we managed to find a shady spot. Dad put the picnic basket down, and Miss J. spread a blanket on the ground.

"Attention, please," boomed a voice. Paula had told me a loudspeaker system would be hooked up, but the voice startled me anyway.

"Will all riders please report to the judging booth? You must sign in and get your number. Please report to the judging booth." It was Mrs. Larrick. I could tell.

"Do you want me to come with you?" asked Mom.

"That's okay. Thanks, Mom. I can find it. . . . Come on, Katie," I added grimly. I hated being in charge of her.

I set off across the field with the Pest. Sara and Carol came along.

The judging booth looked crowded, but we got in line and only had to wait a few minutes.

"Hi, there, Champ," said Paula when we reached the booth.

I grinned.

"Okay . . . Wendy and Katie White." Paula checked off two names on a sheaf of papers attached to a clipboard. "Now step over there to Chris and he'll give you each a number to wear when your class shows."

Chris was sitting behind a table with a stack of cardboard signs on it. Each one had two little holes at the top. Across the middle was a big black number, and under that, in red, were the words RED ROSE FEEDS and a picture of a rose.

"Hey, Wendy! Hey, Cute Stuff! All set for the big show?" Chris handed each of us two safety pins. Then he gave me number *108* and the Pest number *74*. "Pin these to the backs of your shirts, okay? And remember your numbers."

"Okay," we said. The Pest looked as nervous as I felt.

Sara pinned number *108* on my back, while Carol pinned number *74* on the Pest's back.

Then we set out for Mom and Dad and the shade. I looked over my shoulder at the thermometer on the judging booth.

One hundred degrees.

When we reached our spot, Miss J. gave us each a cup of apple juice. Then I read Scottie a story, mostly to keep my mind off my butterflies.

We had almost finished his picture book when Mrs. Larrick came over the loudspeaker again. She announced the order in which the classes were going to show. Our class would be seventh.

That meant we wouldn't show for about two hours. Two *hours*. How could I wait? Those butterflies felt as if they were tap-dancing inside me.

Sara and Carol and I left the shade and went to the ring to watch the first event. It was the other beginners' class. A boy with orange hair and lots of freckles was riding Mr. Chips. Not very well, though. He was hardly even paying attention.

The next event was held on the jumping course. It was an adult class. Mr. Chips was being ridden again, this time by a woman wearing a green riding hat just like mine. She was a good rider. She controlled Mr. Chips well, and he took all the jumps smoothly.

We watched one more event and got so hot we could hardly stand it. I felt damp all over. Sweat was running in my eyes and down my back. And I hadn't been doing anything but standing around.

"Come on, you guys," I said to Sara and Carol. "Let's go get something to drink. Gosh, Mr. Chips must be hot. He's been working hard already, and he's got a few more events to go today. I hope he's not too tired by the time I ride him."

It was twelve-fifteen before Mrs. Larrick called for our class to get ready. The temperature had risen to a hundred and one. Katie and I stood around outside the main riding ring with the other kids, waiting for our horses. One by one, Chris and Paula led them to us.

At last everyone was mounted and ready to go— everyone except me. Where was Mr. Chips?

Paula ran over to me. "Wendy," she said breathlessly. She walked me away from my class. "There's been a . . . a little change. Mr. Chips has been ridden in four events this morning. He's overheated and very tired. We've got to cool him off and let him rest. I'm afraid you can't ride him."

"Oh, no," I cried. "Come on, Paula. Please? Just one more event."

"I'm sorry," she said. "We can't. It's this heat. You don't want Mr. Chips to get sick, do you?"

I shook my head. "Can I ride Daybreak?" I asked desperately.

"Well, no," said Paula. "Mandy's riding her. And here's the thing. The only horse you *can* ride is Sky High—"

"Sky High?" I shrieked.

"Shh," said Paula. "Calm down. It's just that Sky High is the only horse who's free *and* cool. He's been ridden just once today."

"Figures," I said. I turned away from Paula. I didn't want her to see the tears in my eyes. It wasn't fair. It just wasn't fair. There went my chance at winning the first important prize in my whole life. If I had to ride Sky High, and the Pest got to ride gentle Daffodil, she'd beat me for sure.

For several long seconds I struggled against crying. When I was in control of myself, I turned back to Paula. "Okay, where is he?" I demanded.

"On his way. Chris is saddling him up."

I nodded.

And while I waited for Sky High, I made a decision. I decided that I wouldn't let Sky High make

me look bad. I might not win a prize, and I might not ride as well as I'd have ridden Mr. Chips or Peanuts, but I was not going to let Sky High make a fool out of me. Not with my family and friends watching.

When Chris brought Sky High to me, I didn't hesitate. I mounted him as if he were any other horse. Then I walked him to the end of the line our class had formed. When he started to wander off, nibbling grass, I jerked him back. He snorted at me and looked surprised, but he obeyed.

Our class filed into the ring. At Mrs. Larrick's orders, we walked our horses around twice. Then we pulled the line up tight and came to a halt. Mrs. Larrick asked Mandy, who was at the head of the line, to walk her horse around to the other end. When she finished, Vicky followed.

The Pest was next. She kicked at Daffodil and he walked primly around the ring. Katie looked a little shaky, but it was probably just nerves.

When it was my turn, I kicked Sky High twice sharply, and immediately he began walking briskly. Too briskly. And he was heading toward Mrs. Larrick in the center of the ring. I sat up straight and turned him toward the fence. I managed to slow him down, too. Then he behaved beautifully. But I didn't trust him at all.

While the rest of the class took their turns, I concentrated very hard on controlling Sky High. I concentrated so hard that I didn't even see my family and Sara and Carol until I noticed Dad running around with his camera, taking pictures.

We have about a million pictures of the Pest doing wonderful things. Dad has captured her holding up awards, trophies and checks. He's taken her playing the piano, painting at her easel, and coming out the door of the music school. He has photos of her artwork, and pictures of her holding up the newspaper articles she's mentioned in.

There are a couple of cute pictures of me in the hammock and of me smiling after I lost my front teeth, but that's about it. Until now. Now we would have pictures of me riding in a horse show!

Mrs. Larrick asked our class to begin trotting around the ring.

I had to pay attention.

I forgot about Dad and the camera, and kicked Sky High into a trot. He burst forward until his nose was almost touching Sundance's rump. Very calmly, I slowed him down. We trotted along, but not smoothly. I had to work hard to keep him in line and going at the right speed. I couldn't relax for a second. I couldn't even watch Katie to see how she was doing.

At last we stopped the horses. Now we would trot around the ring one at a time. I was able to watch the Pest when she took her turn. She did everything perfectly, except that she steadied herself by resting her hands on the saddle. I hadn't seen her do that in weeks. She must have been awfully nervous.

My turn.

I sighed.

Please don't blow it, Sky High, I thought. Just give me a *little* cooperation. That's all I ask.

I kicked Sky High into a walk. So far, so good.

I kicked him again. And the next thing I knew he was flying around the ring in a wild canter. It was all I could do to stay on. I squeezed in with my knees, leaned forward, and tried to move with his rhythm. When we neared the end of the line, I pulled on the reins good and hard. I wanted him to get the message to STOP.

He did.

But we'd blown it.

Thanks a lot, Sky High. Thanks a whole lot.

I could hardly keep from crying as our class finished up and we filed out of the ring. All my work, all my practicing, all my wishing and hoping were for nothing. Nothing. And all because of some dumb old horse.

Sky High.

He was so rude.

Outside the ring, I dismounted silently and handed Sky High over to Chris.

"You looked good out there, Champ," he said.

"You're kidding."

"No, really. Good control with a difficult horse. The judges will like that."

"Oh, yeah?"

"Yeah." He grinned at me.

But I wasn't so sure. Maybe I'd get an honorable mention, but I couldn't hope for much more. I waited on pins and needles until the winners were announced.

When the judge's voice came over the loudspeaker and said, "And now the winners in the seventh event," I gripped Sara's hand.

"I can't stand it," I wailed. "I'm so nervous!"

Sara smiled at me. "Cross all your fingers and toes," she advised.

I crossed as many as I could.

The judge continued, "Two honorable mentions go to number sixteen and number forty-eight, Victoria Anderson and Mark Vallario."

A cheer arose from a group of people nearby.

"Third prize goes to number one-hundred-eight, Wendy White."

Wendy White? Wendy White! He said my name! "He said my name!" I yelled.

"Second prize," the judge continued, "goes to number ninety-two, Pamela Browning. And first prize goes to number one-twenty, Amanda Stine."

The Pest hadn't won a prize! I'd won and the Pest hadn't! It was almost too much to believe.

I felt myself caught up in one of Dad's big bear hugs. He let me go. Then Mom hugged me and then Miss J. hugged me. Sara and Carol and Scottie were squealing and jumping up and down.

"I won! I won!" I shouted. "I really won!"

I saw the Pest standing quietly apart from our group. She looked uncertain. While I was thinking of something to say to her, Mom took me by the arm. "Come on, sweetheart. They're going to award the prizes now."

As long as I live, I won't forget how I felt when I walked up to that judging booth and let Mrs. Larrick pin the yellow button to my shirt. It had a wide ribbon attached to it which said *third prize* in up and down letters like this:

T   P
H   R
I   I
R   Z
D   E

I grinned and grinned and Dad snapped about a whole roll of film. At the last second, I remembered to thank Mrs. Larrick and the judges. Then I ran back to Mom and Dad.

And the Pest.

She stepped around Mom and said quickly, "Congratulations. I'm glad you won, Wendy."

"Thank you. . . . And I—I'm sorry you didn't." I wasn't. But I was sorry that she was disappointed. I knew how she felt. Believe me.

We had walked back to our spot in the shade and Miss J. was packing up the picnic basket.

"Did Mommy tell you I'm not going to be riding anymore?" Katie asked me.

"No," I answered, surprised, "she didn't."

"Well, I'm not. Riding is okay, I guess, but I'd rather do other things."

I nodded. Inside, I felt like singing and jumping and cheering. No more Katie! No more Pest! Lessons alone! I was very relieved, but I didn't know what to say.

Katie didn't either. She opened her mouth, then closed it.

I felt sort of confused. Katie was still my sister. She was still a Gigantic Pest. And I had just won a small victory. So why did I feel sorry for her? Why did I suddenly wish she felt as happy as I did right now?

I looked over at the others. The picnic basket was packed and ready to go.

"Well, come on," I said to Katie. "It's time to leave."

We followed Mom and Dad, and as we walked I felt the heavy Third Prize button thumping against my chest. I smiled to myself.

That evening, Mom and Dad put my award in a picture frame and stood it on the mantelpiece where anyone could see it. Then Dad took a picture of me standing in front of the fireplace, pointing to the award. Later, when the film was developed, he made two copies of that picture—a little one for our photo album, and a big one for me. Katie made a frame for mine and I hung it over my bed next to the picture of Peanuts she had drawn.

13.

Sniffles

Three days after the horse show was our last day of summer vacation. Carol and Sara and I decided we better use the day as carefully as possible. First we slept late. After breakfast we took a bicycle ride. Then when we were just hot enough and sweaty enough, we rode to Jennifer's house and dove in her pool. Jennifer played Marco Polo and underwater tag with us. Then we took turns jumping on her trampoline, and finally we decided to go to the movies. *The Black Stallion* was playing and we sat through it twice. On the way home, we stopped for ice-cream cones.

As we were leaving the drugstore, licking our double scoops of chocolate mint chip, my eyes fell on the stack of *Riverside Journals*. Right on the front page was a photo of a horse, and underneath it were the words HASTY ACRES HORSE SHOW.

"Hey, you guys! Wait!" I cried.

Carol, Sara, and Jennifer had been halfway out the door, but they turned around and came back in.

"Look at this," I said. "Hasty Acres Horse Show."

"Wow," exclaimed Sara. "What else does it say? Is there an article?"

"It says 'Story on page six'."

Frantically, I thumbed through to page six. I kept looking over my shoulder. I knew that Mr. Campbell, who ran the store, didn't like kids reading his magazines and newspapers without paying for them first.

I spread the *Riverside Journal* open. All of page six was about the horse show. There were several photographs—one of a woman on Daybreak sailing smoothly over a jump, one of a little kid in the other beginners' class with his honorable mention button, and one of Mrs. Larrick in the judging booth.

I scanned the story until I came to a section headed "Winners!"

Carol saw it at the same time. "Look!" She jabbed her finger at the paragraph. "There you are!" she exclaimed.

"What? I'm where?" I began to feel quivery all over.

"The winners in Beginners' Class II," read Carol, "were Amanda Stine, first prize; Pamela Browning, second prize; and Wendy White, third prize. Two honorable mentions—"

"Hey! Oh, let me see!" I grabbed the paper.

There was my name, printed and official. I kept staring at it. *Wendy White*, it said, *third prize*.

"Ahem."

Carol, Sara, Jennifer and I all jumped.

We turned around.

Mr. Campbell was looming over us.

"Are you ready to buy that now?" he asked.

"What? Oh. Oh, yeah. Sure." I fumbled in my pocket for some change, and handed it to Mr. Campbell.

The next thing I knew, Sara was fumbling in *her* pocket for some change. "I'll have one, too," she said grandly. She lifted another paper off the top of the stack.

"Me, too," said Carol.

"Me, too," said Jennifer.

Mr. Campbell stood in front of us looking very surprised. He couldn't think of anything to say. He just watched the four of us flounce out the door with our papers.

As soon as we were on the sidewalk and the door had swung shut behind us, we started giggling.

"You're a star!" cried Sara, putting her arm around me.

"Yeah, you're famous!" said Jennifer.

"A celebrity," added Carol.

"And I bet Mr. Campbell will never bother *us* again," Sara said as we began walking home.

In a little while we reached Jennifer's house. "See you in . . . school . . . tomorrow," she said, choking on the word 'school'.

"Gross," replied Carol and Sara and I. "See you!"

We got on our bikes and rode to our houses.

"I have to help Mom with supper," said Carol.

"And I promised my mother I'd try on last year's school clothes," said Sara.

"Okay. See you tomorrow." We waved good-bye to each other.

I put my bike in the garage and sat glumly on the front porch. I was holding that terrific newspaper article in my hands, but I felt sad and mopey. Today was the end of summer vacation. Tomorrow was school.

Yechh.

I sat there with my chin in my hands. I sat there for so long my bottom began to hurt. And I got the creepy feeling I was being watched. I turned, expecting to see someone standing inside the front door, but no one was there. I looked around the yard. No one there, either.

Suddenly I heard a rustling in the bushes next to the porch.

I began to feel suspicious.

"Katie?" I said sharply.

"Yeah?" She crawled out from the bushes.

Spying again! I couldn't believe it. I was so mad, I could barely speak.

Finally I managed to sputter, "Why do you always *spy* on me? Why can't you *talk* to me like a normal person?"

"Because you never talk to *me* like a normal person." Katie settled herself one step down and looked up at me. "You either yell or tease. Usually you don't speak to me at all."

"And that's because you're always doing dumb things like spying on me or reading my diary or goof-calling me. Why don't you just lay off, Katie? Leave me alone."

Katie's lower lip began to tremble.

"And don't cry," I said. Then I handed her the newspaper article. "You think just because you win awards you're better than me. Well, look at this."

Katie was so surprised that she stopped crying.

"See that? I can get in the paper, too. Just like you."

Katie glanced at me and then read the "winners" paragraph.

By the time she finished, I felt calmer.

So did she.

"Neat," she commented. "I wish I'd gotten in the paper."

"You've *been* in the paper, for heaven's sake! A hundred times."

"Don't be so mad! Anyway, I've only been in the paper four times."

I didn't say anything.

"You know," said Katie. "I can't help the things I do. And I don't do them just to make you angry."

"I know," I said with a sigh, "but you *could* help spying and goof-calling and invading my privacy."

"Yeah," replied Katie. She thought a minute. "And you could be nicer to me. At least, you could be nicer when I'm *not* spying and goof-calling."

"I guess," I said. I gave the Pest a wry smile.

Two-way street, I reminded myself. Maybe the Pest would be less pesty if I helped her be less pesty.

While I was thinking about that, Mom pulled into the driveway.

"Mom! Mom!" I shouted, jumping up and running to the carport. "Look!" I handed her the paper as she got out of the car. "Read this!"

Mom put down her briefcase. She looked at the

headline and the photographs. Then she read the paragraph where my name was printed.

"Oh, Wendy," she said. "I'm so proud of you." She put her arms around me and gave me a great big hug. "I hope you're proud of yourself."

"Oh, I am, Mom. I'm going to take this to school tomorrow and show it to my new teacher."

"Okay. Now listen, you two. Why don't you run and find Scottie. Dad'll be home in a few minutes and we've got a surprise for you."

Katie and I took off like a shot. We practically forgot about our fight.

The surprise turned out to be a puppy!

When Dad got home, he and Mom and Katie and Scott and I sat down in the living room.

"Well," said Dad, "your mother and I have done some thinking this summer. We know you've been wanting a pet."

For just one exciting second, even after all that had happened, I thought my parents might have changed their minds and decided to get a horse.

But Dad continued, "We think you're old enough to be responsible for a pet. A horse wasn't the right pet for us—"

I didn't even feel disappointed. I really knew they weren't getting a horse.

"So," Dad said, "we thought a dog might be the next best thing."

"A dog?" cried Scottie, jumping up. "A dog! A dog! Oh, boy!"

Mom and Dad smiled.

"How would you like to go to the pet store at Clover Mall tonight and pick out a puppy?" asked Mom.

"Oh, yes!" cried Katie.

"All *right!*" I shouted.

So after dinner we got in the station wagon and drove to the mall. And that was how, the day before school began this year, we got Sniffles—a roly-poly, wiggly cocker spaniel who likes to lick our faces.

That night I fell asleep thinking about the newspaper article, with Sniffles cuddled up on my stomach.

14.

The Guinness Book of World Records

"Ew, ew!" shrieked Katie.

"Yikes, I'm glad I put on my bathing suit!" shouted Scott.

"I'm soaked!" I giggled.

It was a Saturday at the end of September, and I'd just come back from working at Hasty Acres. It was probably one of the last really hot days we'd have until next summer.

Mom and Dad asked us to wash Miss J.'s car for her. We were soapy and wet. So was Sniffles. He was running in and out of our feet, jumping and yapping. He liked being squirted with the hose.

Katie soaped up the windshield. I aimed the hose and sprayed the soap off. Then I stuck my finger over the end of the hose and showered Katie.

Spluttering and giggling, she pulled a sponge out of a bucket of cold water and threw it at my head. I ducked and the sponge hit Scott.

"I'm gonna get you!" he yelled. He dumped a little pail of water over me. I had to stand still and crouch down to let him but I don't think he cared.

As I was drying my face with one of the car-washing rags, Sara came charging out of her back-yard and onto our driveway. She was waving an envelope.

"Look, look, look, look, look!" she shouted. "Wendy, look at this!"

"What?" I asked.

"Oh, I can *not* believe it!"

I finished drying myself off. Sara handed me the envelope. I pulled a letter out.

It was from the people at *The Guinness Book*.

My hands began to shake.

I read the letter very slowly so I'd be sure to understand every word.

The letter said that we had set a record. Our saga was the longest poem ever written in America by kids under twelve. And when the new *Guinness Book* was published, our names would be in it!

"It must be a joke," I said.

"It's not," replied Sara. "At least I don't think is."

For a long time we stared at each other. Then I grabbed Sara and hugged her.

"Where's Carol? Does she know?" I asked.

"She's not home. We'll have to tell her later."

"Katie!" I said. "Did you hear? We're going to be in *The Guinness Book!*" I didn't wait for her to answer. I was too excited. "I've got to go tell Mom and Dad. I wonder if anyone else in Riverside ever set a record that was in *The Guinness Book.*"

"Hey, maybe we'll be in the paper," said Sara.

"Oh, yeah. Wow, that would be twice in one month . . ."

I grinned. I was thinking about the summer. About riding and Peanuts and Paula and the horse show and the saga and the newspaper article and Katie and Sniffles and working at Hasty Acres. Maybe I would be mentioned in the paper again.

Ho hum. Another newspaper article about me. Two in one month. I guess I can live with it!

About the Author

ANN M. MARTIN grew up in Princeton, New Jersey, and is a graduate of Smith College. Her Apple paperbacks are *Yours Turly, Shirley; Ten Kids, No Pets; With You and Without You; Me and Katie (the Pest); Stage Fright; Inside Out; Bummer Summer;* and the books in THE BABY-SITTERS CLUB series and the BABY-SITTERS LITTLE SISTER series.

Ms. Martin lives in New York City with her cat, Mouse. She likes ice cream and *I Love Lucy;* and she hates to cook.

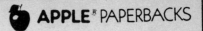